TRAITOR

GUDRUN PAUSEWANG

Translated by Rachel Ward

Andersen Press • London

First published in English in 2004 by
Andersen Press Limited,
20 Vauxhall Bridge Road, London SWIV 2SA
www.andersenpress.co.uk

Original title: *Die Verräterin*
© 1995 by Ravensburger Buchverlag
English translation © 2004 by Rachel Ward

All rights reserved. No part of this publication may be reproduced,
stored in a retrieval system, or transmitted in any form or by any
means, electronic, mechanical, photocopying, recording or
otherwise, without the written permission of the publisher.

British Library Cataloguing in Publication Data available

ISBN 1 84270 313 7

MORAY COUNCIL LIBRARIES & INFO.SERVICES	
2O 12 55 55	
Askews	
J C Y	

Typeset by FiSH Books, London WC1
Printed and bound in Great Britain by Mackays of Chatham Ltd.,
Chatham, Kent

1

Mellersdorf. The train stopped. Anna got out, and with her a few other people, almost all school children who were coming home for the weekend. Also an old woman. And two soldiers, probably on leave.

Dusk was already falling. The snow crunched. Hardly any light fell from the station buildings.

There was a strictly enforced blackout, so as not to offer any target to the enemy aeroplanes. Air-raid defence – words that every child knew now.

Anna hated the station with the desolate, smoky waiting room; above all she hated the bleak light of the ceiling lamps which made everyone waiting there look like corpses. Every Saturday afternoon she arrived here, and she left again from here every Sunday evening. And from here to Stiegnitz was still another two kilometres.

Stiegnitz. A hole at the end of the world. Why didn't she live in Schonberg like most of the rest of her classmates? Why did she only have an attic room with the Beraneks there in the town? Everything interesting in the world happened in Schonberg, not in Stiegnitz. Dancing classes for example. And the theatre. And the cinema. And the Café Paris was there too, directly opposite her school, on the Adolf-Hitler-Strasse. Girls from the grammar school always sat there, it was a popular meeting place, she liked it there.

She trudged around the station and set off into the forest, which stretched from Mellersdorf to Stiegnitz, with her schoolbag in one hand, and the bag with her dirty washing in the other. It had snowed that afternoon. She was leaving tracks. The sky was clear now though, and still a little bit red in the west.

There was a footpath through the valley, a shortcut along the banks of the stream.

Anna heard the rushing water. The stream seldom froze, as its current was strong. On both banks cushions of snow were piling up, patterned with birds' tracks. A hare had hopped along the bank too. And a human track crossed over the snow between the stream and the path. Anna often came across deer and squirrel tracks in this valley. And it wasn't uncommon for foxes to hang around here. Seff, her older brother, had taught her a long time ago to recognise which tracks belonged to which animals.

As a small child she had been afraid of the valley because the forest was so dark and the stream roared so loudly. And because people said that ghosts lived here. All the tracks on either side of this path that she hadn't been able to interpret, she had put down to ghosts. Until Seff had laughingly explained every single one of them to her.

Then suddenly the fear was gone. And since Anna had been going to school in Schonberg, this path between Mellersdorf and Stiegnitz had long ago become an everyday thing to her. If she had wanted to wonder about all the prints in the snow that she had already come across, it would have kept her busy! But some really did pose a puzzle. Hadn't she just seen tracks from men's shoes, which led from the stream to the path? Here on the path there were five or six different sets of overlapping prints, going towards Stiegnitz – and going towards Mellersdorf. But these tracks were different – with a nick on the left shoe!

Where had the man got to? She turned around. Nothing to see. She put her two bags down and went a couple of steps back.

Now she saw it: the track, coming out of the stream, crossed the path and disappeared into the forest.

What had the man – with his shoes on – been looking for in the stream? Why had he struck out afterwards into the forest?

Anna peered over to the other bank. But it was already too dim to be able to make anything out in the snow there. She turned back to her two bags and wandered on, her thoughts back in the town of Schonberg again.

There was only one thing that she didn't like there: that people everywhere were always talking about politics. Everything was saturated in it; you couldn't avoid it; at school, at the German Girls' League evening meetings, at ceremonies, in newsreels and bookshops. Such words as *Fatherland* and *Immortal*, *Common Destiny* and *Shoulder to Shoulder*, *Unconditional* and *Ultimate Victory* were constantly hammered into you. But there were other things in life still. For example, listening to records and leafing through fashion magazines, reading and watching films. You had to listen to the speeches by Goebbels, Göring and the *Führer* of course. That went without saying. But after a quarter of an hour at most, she could no longer listen to the voices from the radio, which were loud and often got carried away. That was awful, she was afraid that would happen every time! Sometimes however, she was simply overcome by tiredness when the speeches went on and on. Then she supported her chin on her hands and covered her mouth with her fingers so that nobody could see her yawns. At first she had thought that the listening only affected her like that. But the girl who sat next to her had secretly admitted to Anna that she often fought against sleep too. Since then Anna hadn't felt so guilty.

Here in Stiegnitz, her little village, politics and propaganda weren't so important. There the people were far more interested in what was happening in the village. And how promising the harvest looked. And why Blaze, the cow, had been giving less milk for a week and Schimmel, the white horse, was lame. And for Grandmother, and the other old people, the most important thing was still what the priest said, and for the farmers it was what the weather was like.

Of course people in Stiegnitz listened to the news too. But they took what could be heard from their 'People's Radios' calmly. *Führers*, *Kaisers*, kings and presidents came and went, wars alternated with times of peace, people lived and died. And if the *Führer* wanted his ceremonies, then he could have them. People made an effort.

A screech owl cried nearby. Anna jumped. Funny. Had the man waded along the stream, or had he only crossed it? Why hadn't he used the wooden footbridge back there near the last houses in Mellersdorf? Or the bridge just before Stiegnitz? The man must be a stranger here.

She was getting cold and she was hungry. Grandmother would be bound to have something good in the oven. As always.

Once again Anna's thoughts went back to the footprints. Why on earth hadn't the man stayed on the footpath so as to reach the next village as quickly as possible? With his wet feet he risked getting quite a cold!

Between the tall spruces it was nearly dark already. Perhaps he was standing there and peering at her on the path. An unpleasant idea. She wished Seff was by her side.

He would definitely laugh at her, would ask her: Haven't you got anything better to do than to think about something like that?

And he would be right. She decided to forget about the track and trudged on.

Certainly she was somebody here in Stiegnitz. Namely the daughter of the owner of the inn The White Lamb. It was the biggest inn in the place, with a couple of guest rooms upstairs, which all smelled a little musty. That was probably because of the thick walls that were supposed to be centuries old. Everybody knew the landlady of the Lamb, not just in Stiegnitz, but in the whole area. Marie Hanisch, the widow. A capable woman, who had the business of the Lamb firmly under control, even in these times when all the male helpers were at the Front. Even Seff, Anna's older brother. In these times when you couldn't get a single spoonful of quark, a single globule of fat in your soup, without a coupon from a ration card. And when the police stuck their noses into everything! For example, on farms where it happened to smell of sausage soup: Had the slaughtered pig been registered, had the slaughter been permitted? Or in houses where workers from the east and French prisoners of war were working. Were they being treated too kindly? Or in the inn bars: Had someone let fall a disparaging remark about the *Führer* or the Party?

Anna pictured her mother: small, plump, always full of energy, always on the move. Dark hair, a bun at her neck, dimples in her cheeks. She was popular. People met in the Lamb, it was the rumour-exchange. You learned quicker there than elsewhere that Lena was pregnant by Albert, who'd copped it on the Eastern Front two months ago. And that cake mix could be eked out with coffee grounds. And that over in Czechoslovakia, in the Protectorate, there were pickled gherkins for sale – without coupons. And that Toni Wockler, who was allowed to stay at home since they had shot one of his legs off in Italy, sometimes turned the radio dial so carelessly that it ended up on an enemy station. What had he heard there, the good Toni? That the war would soon be over, for example. Of course that was all enemy propaganda! But before the talk came round to this topic, Mother always assured herself that only trustworthy acquaintances, absolutely dependable people, were in the bar.

Many people also let Mother advise and help them. How best to formulate a death notice. Where you could get a good laying hen. And whether, with her connections, she couldn't do something for old Jansa, who wanted to visit his daughter in Trbi, in Czechoslovakia but, as a Czech, couldn't get permission.

Indeed, Mother had very good connections in a lot of places, and was glad to help. After all her brother, Uncle Franz, was mayor of Stiegnitz. The villagers of Stiegnitz knew that she had been called Brünner, not Hanisch, for a long time now. But Felix Brünner, her husband, was long since dead, and Marie came from the respected family of the Hanisches after all.

This respect was carried over to the children. Anna remembered that the village teacher, Herr Schroller, had always been more polite to her than to Trude Fischer, who had a drunken woodsman for a father.

It was now beginning to get dark on the path. Nonetheless, Anna spotted the track which led out from the spruces. No doubt about it, it was the same: the worn down heels, the soles with practically no tread, and then the nick. It wasn't difficult to recognise the pattern again. And then the trail disappeared back into the forest.

While Anna walked on, she fished her torch out of her schoolbag and lit up the snow in front of the spruces. The beam of light wandered along between the path and the edge of the forest. If the track should lead back onto the path again, then she couldn't fail to see it.

Her thoughts began to wander again. Stiegnitz. A miserable dump. There wasn't even a cinema here. If you wanted to see a film, you had to footslog it over to Mellersdorf. There in an empty barn stood a couple of wooden benches, a screen was hung up, and in the background whirred the film equipment, which a war invalid carried from village to village. And that was only in the summer six months. In Schonberg, however, there were actually two proper cinemas, summer and winter!

She heard steps crunching in the snow. Voices became louder. It was two boys trudging from Stiegnitz to Mellersdorf, friends of her younger brother Felix.

'Have you met anybody?' she asked.

No, they hadn't come across anyone. Why did she ask?

She shrugged her shoulders. Just because. Then she asked after Felix, and learned that he was helping in the Lamb. It was very busy there today. A dozen people. Policemen. With dogs. People said they had searched the bunkers.

Anna wanted to ask who or what the people were looking for, but the boys were in a hurry. They had already disappeared into the dark.

The bunkers. She thought of the Moserwald Bunker on the opposite slope, further up, in the middle of the forest. She knew it well. A couple of years ago, when the German soldiers had marched into the Sudetenland, into the predominantly German-speaking border area of Czechoslovakia, it had lost its gun turrets. They had been blown up by German demolition squads, like the gun turrets of all the other former Czech bunkers. These concrete fortresses – built in the mid 1930s as a particularly heavy line of defence along the border with Germany – were no longer needed by anybody since the Czechs had given them up to the Germans without a fight. Anyone who wanted to could wander around in them now.

She had done that. Once she had even gone with Seff along the wide main corridor deep inside the bunker. With a stable lamp. On the way back they had even braved the passages branching off at the sides, had ventured into ever more distant rooms, had only found the way back to the main corridor with difficulty. How far this military installation reached into the hillside couldn't be seen from the entrance because that was nothing more than a rectangle full of darkness between the spruces and the undergrowth of elder. The gravel path which used to lead there was no longer there. After all, who wanted to visit a disused bunker? Only woodsmen, mushroom gatherers and berry pickers came past it sometimes. Perhaps curious children dared to go a few steps down the main corridor now and again. But it was pitch black in there. Without a lamp you were lost.

Anna had felt magically attracted to the bunker entrance back then. The darkness and the silence, the resounding echo, the empty rooms deep in the mountain – she had wanted to explore all that once more, without even Seff. For with him she had only hurried through the bunker, always making an effort not to stumble and to keep up with him. But then, when she had wanted to explore the bunker alone, equipped with a lamp, she had only dared to go into the rooms close to the entrance. She looked round these very closely. Even now, she could still hear the drips that had fallen from the concrete ceiling, and the howling of the wind in the ventilation shafts. In some rooms there was standing water, in others Anna had climbed over scattered rubble. And everywhere inky darkness reigned, apart from the rooms which led to the former gun-ports. The holes blasted in their ceilings let dim light fall to the floor, and for a whole summer Anna had made herself at home in one of these half-lit rooms, made herself a sort of table out of branches and boards and even dragged an old chair from home up there. And she had built a bed out of twigs, hay and moss.

In this bunker room she had sometimes written poems during the holidays, and she had always remained undisturbed. The hay from the bed had been carried away by animals in the meantime, of course, but the jam jar with the bunch of heather in it still stood on the table. After two and a half years. In that summer she had been thirteen, only a few months younger than Felix was now.

Wait! There it was again, the track! It appeared between thick bushes and kept to the edge of the path. The onion-shaped tower of Stiegnitz church could already be seen against the sky and a dimmed streetlamp shimmered. Just ahead there, by the bridge, the path turned off to the little farm with pointed gables, which lay on the edge of the forest, alone and somewhat raised. That was her home.

She was really very hungry. In the early afternoon she

had had another sports lesson at the League. Apparatus gymnastics. That had been exhausting. Now she was looking forward to what Grandmother would have waiting for her. Probably sweet dumplings filled with plum jam. That was her favourite dish.

Clouds were coming up again from the west. The evening bell was ringing. The last one. All the others had already been melted down for the war. Well, so what? Guns were more important now. Seff had written that as well, when Grandmother had complained about the bells in her letters to him.

Oh yes, she had to write to Seff. The army post took a long time sometimes, and it was Christmas in three weeks. A single track ran towards the house. A man's trail. Uncle Franz? No, he would surely still be busy at this time. Had someone come to visit? Perhaps Seff, on leave? Her heart began to hammer. Seff – that was inconceivable!

But then she remembered the trail from earlier again, the other, peculiar one. She had totally forgotten about it! She now turned the beam from the torch directly onto the prints in the snow.

What in the world could a man with wet feet – no, he must be wet up to far over his knees! – be looking for at her house? Who was he?

Anna no longer heard the bell ringing, forgot the bunker, just followed the track. It led to just before the farmyard, swerved into the bushes but then appeared again and vanished into the barn door.

With a racing heart, Anna put both her bags down,

took her torch without switching it on, and stared at the barn. What if that was the man that the guests in the Lamb were looking for! But who were they looking for?

Then a thought struck her: it could only be one of the inmates of the Institute in Sternberg. Now and again it happened that mentally disturbed people escaped from there. Twice before men had been caught in the woods round here. Poor devils who didn't understand the world any more. They would be capable of wading through a stream in the middle of winter.

She took a deep breath. How would the police treat this person when they got him? Someone who couldn't help the way that he was?

She thought about Wenzel Krause. He was eighteen years old, had a friendly grin for everyone and couldn't do anything except chopping wood and suchlike.

He wouldn't hurt a fly and was grateful for every smile. Anna had often stepped in when children ran after him, mimicked him and fooled about behind his back. Someone like Wenzel Krause couldn't defend himself. To hunt someone like that seemed dreadful to her.

So if it was a man from the Institute then, who had fled into the barn, first of all he would need some hot tea and something dry to put on.

Anna crept up to the door, opened it carefully centimetre by centimetre so that it didn't creak, and scurried on tiptoes into the dark space.

Garden equipment, baskets and buckets, boxes and canisters stood in here. All rubbish that wasn't usually needed in winter. And a lot of it wasn't needed at all any more. The old butter barrel, or the snowshoes made of staves for example. Anna's glance slid up the wooden staircase. But it was too dark to be able to make anything out. Up there was just hay, which had lain there for years. Since Grandfather's death, Grandmother had no longer kept cows, just goats. The hay that was kept under the stable roof was enough for them.

Anna listened carefully. Nothing moved. She dared to direct the beam from her torch onto the stairs. There she discovered wet tracks on the steps.

He was up there then. He had probably crept into the hay like a frightened animal.

Very quietly she crept up the stairs. On the fourth step she stopped and listened. She saw nothing, but heard quiet, rapid breathing. Someone with a temperature would breathe like that. The poor devil – how long must they have hunted him? Making every effort to avoid all noise, she climbed up further.

She didn't want to startle him. She just wanted to see where he was lying and what he looked like. Perhaps he was as young as Wenzel? Or perhaps he was already old? But then he wouldn't have made it this far.

Now she stood on the wooden floor and held her breath. The torch shook in her hand. It was a bit creepy really, the whole thing. She heard his breathing again. He must be lying there under the sloping roof timbers, deep in the hay. Carefully she let the beam of light wander. She discovered the sole of a boot, saw the heel that had come off, the tread that was hardly recognisable, the nick. She gathered up all her courage and took two steps forwards.

And one more. Now her torchlight reached him, she could see him lying there.

She turned the beam away from his face, avoided dazzling him. All the same, she could see enough. No, he wasn't an old man, probably not even thirty. And you couldn't tell by looking at him that he was mentally disturbed. But how ill he must be! He lay there in the hay like a corpse: eyes closed and deep in their sockets, sunken and stubbly cheeks, bald head. In such Institutions the patients obviously had their heads shaved. Poor man. Sweat stood out on his brow. He couldn't be left like that. And he had to get back on his feet before the police took him and got him back to Sternberg.

But perhaps he didn't even want to be there? Perhaps he hadn't been so disturbed for a while and he felt that that wasn't his home? Perhaps he could remember his family? And above all, he didn't look like Wenzel Krause. Everyone had always known that Wenzel Krause would never be able to attend school.

Anna slid down the stairs again. Light shimmered across the yard from the living room window. In there was Grandmother. Should she tell her about the man in the barn?

Grandmother would get into a panic, clap her hands over her head and run straight to Uncle Franz to tell him everything. Then he would have no choice but to inform the people in the Lamb immediately. Then they would come with their dogs.

And Mother? She would probably pass the problem over to her brother Franz as well. And Felix? The first thing he would do would be to chase the half-dead man out of the hay himself, drive him into the Lamb and play the role of the hero there, like a big kid.

No. Not that. The poor fellow should have a bit of peace for once.

Get well. Come to himself. Then they could see what to do next.

She picked up the two bags and ran into the house. She didn't even stop in the hallway to take off her shoes, with clumps of snow still sticking to them. Grandmother would be waiting! She stormed into the warm, brightly lit living room.

2

'Sweet Jesus,' Grandmother called out to her. 'What kept you? I thought something had happened.'

'What could happen?' asked Anna, as she took off her coat, threw it over a chair and sat down at the table. 'Did you think that the man they're looking for had attacked me?'

'You already know about it?' exclaimed Grandmother, surprised. 'Where did you hear that?'

Anna told her about Felix's friends that she had met.

'I suppose they had to dish all that straight up to you!' complained Grandmother. 'I didn't want to tell you about it. How are you supposed to walk through the forest to Mellersdorf now, without dying of fear?' She bent down and glanced under the table. 'You wouldn't starve if you stopped to take your shoes off first you know!'

She opened the oven. At once the wonderful smell of sweet dumplings, which Anna loved so much, filled the room. She went out and came back into the room wearing slippers. In here, everything was the same as ever. The advent wreath over the table caught her eye.

'Has Seff written?' she asked. That was always one of her first questions.

Grandmother nodded. 'All leave cancelled,' she sighed.

And then it was the time for her news. She had been into the town with Felix to buy him shoes. One size bigger than necessary. Already a man's size! But how he was growing! And he wasn't even fourteen yet! And Karl Weber had been killed and so had Schroller, the teacher. And old Jeschken had broken her leg.

Anna wasn't listening. In her thoughts, she was in the barn. She drank three mugs of malt coffee, but only ate two dumplings. She realised that in any case, she had to leave again by tomorrow evening at the latest, to get to Schonberg for school. Would the man be in good enough shape by then to be able to walk on alone? And if not – what then? What would happen to him while she wasn't there? After all, he was ill, he might become noisy up there, give himself away...

Grandmother was surprised. 'Is something wrong?'

Anna crammed another dumpling.

'You mustn't be afraid,' said Grandmother and stroked Anna's hair. 'They'll have him safe by tomorrow evening. The other seven have already been caught.'

'There were eight?' cried Anna in amazement.

Grandmother nodded. 'Only the eighth is still running around free.'

'And the other seven? What have they done with them?'

'All shot while attempting to escape, so they say.'

Anna stared into space. Seven men shot while trying to escape. That was inhuman! You couldn't expect mentally disturbed people to stand still when you ordered them to! Were the ones who escaped really so dangerous that they had to shoot at them? Anna couldn't understand that. The sleeper over there in the barn didn't look dangerous at any rate. And then she thought: to shoot someone while they were attempting to escape wasn't fair.

Of course the man who had escaped onto their farm would also try to run away if he felt he had been driven into a corner. Then would they shoot him down too?

No, no, no! She didn't want to be in any way implicated in that! How they treated such ill people! As if they were rubbish.

'And if that fellow is still free tomorrow, then Felix will go with you to Mellersdorf,' comforted Grandmother.

Felix! He was still almost a child. Someone like that would soon blow him away. Felix wasn't afraid though. He would go for him at once. He could hardly wait to become a soldier. He was very worried that the war would be over before he, Felix, was old enough to be able to join in.

If only she could take him into her confidence. After all, he was there all week. But she wouldn't be able to win him over for something like that. Mentally disturbed people were just dead-weight for him too. That was what they learned at school and in the Hitler Youth. Help him to stay alive? What for? He just eats and serves no purpose!

Anna saw things differently. She hadn't let herself be spoon-fed with everything they were taught at League meetings until she believed everything unconditionally. There were some things that she doubted. That humanity was made out of valuable and less valuable races, for example. And that the Jewish race was so inferior that you had to fight them like pest-control officers did with bugs! She could still remember the Grünbaums. The general store in Stiegnitz had belonged to them. They had been nice people who gave sweets to the children, and if money was tight for somebody, they gave him time to pay.

Also, in Anna's opinion, it wasn't right that Hitler had taken Czechoslovakia, without asking the Czechs if that was what they wanted. It was just occupied and put under 'German protection', and that was that! Then it was called the 'Protectorate'. If she were a Czech, then she wouldn't exactly love the Germans!

Nonetheless, her feelings towards the *Führer* were not disapproving on principle. He was not only the conqueror, he had other things to offer as well. He had taken back the Sudetenland and united Austria with Germany, Germans with Germans. And families with lots of children were made much of. And the mothers were honoured . . .

Grandmother was still guided more by her Jesus than by Hitler. And Mother too let fall a critical remark now and then, when she was at home, and Felix wasn't there. And Frau Beranek, her landlady in Schonberg, had sometimes grumbled very specifically about this state of affairs. But only if nobody else could be listening.

That was another thing. Why weren't you allowed to say openly what you thought?

She remembered Sonja, who sat next to her. Once, after a trip to the cinema together, she had told her a poem under the seal of secrecy, which, so she said, was secretly doing the rounds. It went like this: Ten little

grumblers were together drinking wine, one scoffed:
'Goebbels – what a fool!' then there were only nine.
Nine little grumblers sat thinking till quite late, one
shared his doubts with someone else, then there were
only eight. Eight little grumblers muttered, 'God in
heaven...!' but one of them was overheard, then there
were only seven. Seven little grumblers found they were
in a fix: when one complained about the food then there
were only six. And so on. The last two verses went: The
last one let this verse be found by loyal Party men, who
shipped him off to Dachau too – and there were ten
again! So Adolf thought, 'I've got you now! You can't
escape!' he thundered. But by this time, where ten had
been were now another hundred!

It was a poem that had made an immediate impression
on Anna. After repeating it to herself several times, she
had it in her head. The fifth little grumbler disappeared
because he had played Mendelssohn on the piano. Who
Mendelssohn had been, she had found out since then: a
Jewish composer. But for a long time, Dachau had
remained a secret dark spot in her imagination. Sonja
didn't know what all that about Dachau meant either.
But it was clear that this poem was very, very dangerous
and that you should only recite it to people that you were
absolutely sure of. She, Anna, had once whispered it to
Mother, when they were in the cellar preparing the seed-
potatoes. It had left Mother speechless. And Anna had
had to promise there and then absolutely never, never
again to recite the poem to anyone at all. But all the
same, Anna had learned from her what Dachau meant:

there was a concentration camp there for the politically unreliable. That was 'little grumblers' and such people.

It had started with that poem. She had begun to think about things. And she had carried on thinking. The Ultimate Victory, for example, which the *Führer* was always talking about – was it worth so many lives?

Above all, it seemed to her that Hitler, and all those who had the say at the moment, were too careless with human life.

She saw the face before her, the face of the man in the hay. One should have pity on him – whoever he was. In any case, he was a human being.

She shook her head. Crazy world. If it was a half-dead dog lying there in the hay, Felix would be the first to struggle to keep him alive!

She started. When Felix came home, he too would discover the trail of a strange man in the snow! And soon he'd be in the barn and would be snooping around in the hay!

'Something's not right with you,' said Grandmother and looked at her sharply. 'Only three dumplings! Is there something else on your mind?'

'I think I'm getting a cold,' said Anna. 'Will you make me some hot milk? Make me a whole jugful. I'll take it to my room. And can you put some honey in it?'

'Why didn't you say that straight away?' exclaimed Grandmother and she got busy. Anna got her jug of hot milk and honey, and Grandmother advised her to go straight to bed.

'Sleep yourself better!' she called up the stairs after her.

She always said that in such situations. Anna waited until Grandmother had disappeared back into the living room, then she slipped into her old rubber boots and darted into the yard with the full jug, the torch in her skirt pocket. It was snowing in big, thick flakes. There was practically nothing left to see of either her own track or the strange one.

Thank God.

Over in the living room, the radio was humming. That was good, thought Anna.

With a racing heart she crept up the stairs. She let the beam from the torch wander over the hay above her until she had the soles of the shoes in the light. The man was still sleeping. He couldn't drink the milk in his sleep. She would have to wake him carefully. But what if he then began to shout in panic?

The problem solved itself more quickly than she had expected. The jug was getting too heavy for her to carry with one hand. In the attempt to put it down on a rafter, the beam from the torch accidentally flickered across the man's eyes. Shocked, he jumped up. In consternation Anna let the torch fall and pressed the jug to her chest. If only he wouldn't make any noise now! And she didn't even have a free hand to put her finger to her lips!

But he only stared at her with wide-open eyes. She saw that his chin was shaking. That gave her the courage to put the torch on the rafter, still switched on, and hand him the jug. The milk was steaming. He drank without putting it down. He spilled a bit in the process. Through the steam, she saw his large shining eyes, whose gaze was directed at her.

What odd clothes he had on. Some kind of army coat. The question: Why isn't he wearing Institution things? shot through her head. Strange. But she was too nervous to think about it for long.

He passed the jug back to her. She nodded to him, smiling: Don't be afraid, my dear, you'll be welcome here. Even as Napoleon, or whatever you think you are.

While she was bending over him to take the jug, he stretched out his hand and laid it carefully on the back of her hand, just for a moment. She hardly felt the touch. But she did feel the feverish heat.

This attempt to thank her was moving. If he was still capable of saying thank you, then he couldn't be completely crazy. And the police were spending so much time and energy on this poor man? How peculiar.

She took the torch from the rafter, reached for the jug, laid her finger on her lips and nodded to the man. Then she darted down the stairs and into the house. She made it upstairs and into her room without Grandmother noticing anything from the living room.

It was warm in here. Grandmother had already stoked up the iron stove. It smelled of pine resin, of home. The Beraneks' attic in Schonberg couldn't be heated, the most she could do there was to plug in an electric fire. Or go down to Frau Beranek in the sitting room.

She forced herself now for the first time to think about what she should do next. Worrying about what should happen now with the refugee out there, could wait till later. Somehow she would manage to hide him from the police and their dogs. When it had blown over a bit, considered Anna, then she would speak to Mother – and ask her advice about how the man could be brought back to Sternberg unobtrusively.

The hot milk had done him good. But he still had the wet trousers and wet boots on. Enough grounds for Grandmother to prophesy pneumonia – if she knew about it. It almost seemed as if he'd got pneumonia already. She couldn't leave him lying there like that.

She slipped into the boys' room next door and opened Seff's wardrobe. All his civilian clothes that she knew so well were hanging there. She checked, considered, compared, then decided on the old corduroy trousers, a faded loden jacket, a vest, the pullover with the darned elbows – all things that Seff would hardly miss if he came home unexpectedly. She also fished a pair of socks out of a drawer, but shoes – they stood downstairs in the hall. Grandmother always had her eye on them. If Seff's boots were missing, she'd notice that at once. No, she couldn't provide shoes for the poor chap.

The radio was still on in the living room. Anna took the torch, slipped into her coat, wrapped it over Seff's clothes and ran through the snow flurries over to the barn. If Grandmother should catch her running across the yard, she'd just say: 'Before Christmas there are a lot of secrets . . .'

He was waiting for her, half sitting up. His features were distorted, his eyes full of fear. But when he recognised her, his face relaxed. She handed him the things, held her finger to her lips again to warn him, and hurried back into the house. Back in her room again, she crawled into bed.

No, the man in the hay was not as crazy as Wenzel Krause. He got most of what was going on around him. Pretty much everything really. Despite the fever. What had driven him mad?

Noises sounded from downstairs, doors opened and closed, Felix's high-pitched laughter rang out. Mother and Felix had come home. She heard light, fast footsteps on the stairs. And soon the door opened. Felix. He was always like that: thoughtless in dealing with others. Rash. It didn't occur to him that she might be asleep.

'Have you heard?' he asked and sat down on the edge of her bed. His cheeks were glowing with excitement. 'They were on a Russian-hunt here. They've got seven already. The eighth is hiding somewhere. He can't be far...'

Anna started up. Her pulse was racing. 'What?' she shouted. 'Russians?'

He looked at her in amazement. 'What did *you* think then?'

'Mentally disturbed people,' she answered quietly. 'From the Institute in Sternberg...'

He began to laugh. 'Lunatics!' he shouted and clapped his hands on his thighs. 'That's a joke. Madmen! What would be the point of that? It wouldn't be the first time. And there wouldn't be so much fuss about them. But Russians! Real Russians! Broken out of a prisoner of war camp near Glatz. Last Tuesday. They bagged the sixth and seventh this morning. If I gave the last one up to the police, I'd be in the paper, Anna! And all of you too, as my family. Perhaps there's even a medal for something like that. In any case, that would be a deed for the Fatherland to be proud of!'

'You've got to get him first,' said Anna dryly, her heart beating like mad. 'The Russian is hardly going to come up to you and say: Here I am.'

'You're not taking me seriously,' he said, annoyed.

'I don't feel well,' she murmured, letting herself sink back and turning towards the wall. 'Let me sleep now.'

She tried to get her thoughts in order. A Russian. She'd never seen a real Russian before. Only in pictures, or in the newsreels. French prisoners of war were working in Stiegnitz and nearly every farmer round here had a worker from the east: a Pole or a Ukrainian. And in Schonberg she had once meet a troop of captured Englishmen. But a Russian? Never!

'Do you want the light on or off?' she heard Felix ask from the door. In his voice there was a tone of awkwardness, embarrassment, tenderness. But he was so distant.

'Off.'

So he switched off the light and whispered, 'Get well soon!'

And after a few seconds of silence: 'Did you hear? Get well soon!'

'Out!' shouted Anna. 'You're getting on my nerves!'

He shut the door so quietly that she hardly heard it, and crept down the stairs.

3

She rolled over onto her back and stared at the ceiling. So he was a Russian. A Russian prisoner of war, on the run. Someone who could no longer stand being held prisoner. One of the Russian *Soldateska* who attacked women, killed children, tortured old people to death, in short: someone with blood on his hands. She still had a very clear memory of the placard showing an angry man's snarling face, with a Russian military cap and a knife dripping with blood between his clenched teeth, instilling fear in the viewer. And it wasn't all that long since the photos of Nemmersdorf had been in the papers, the village in East Prussia, which the Russian army had overrun out of the blue, in a surprise attack. When the Germans had taken it back a short time afterwards, they discovered that almost all the inhabitants had been murdered: children, women, old people – with hideous injuries. They had been terrible photos that she would never forget. How can people do such things? She had asked herself that at the time, and was still asking.

And she had wanted to save the life of someone like that!

No, no way. She must speak to Mother at once, inform the police. He was an enemy and belonged in a prison camp. That conditions weren't exactly luxurious in there went without saying. He would just have to see it through. He just mustn't try to escape. Then he wouldn't get shot.

But something made her think again. She thought of the word Felix had used: bagged. She shuddered. That was unthinkable for her too: to treat a person like an animal. Even if it was a Russian.

And were *all* Russians really such brutes? The man up there didn't look like that at all. She thought about his moving way of thanking her, saw again the mortal fear in his eyes, his miserable condition. They had hunted him although he was half-starved. But they still hadn't been able to 'bag' him.

But to hide a Russian, that was treachery. So she would be a traitor if she didn't betray him at once.

But then – wouldn't she be his murderer?

Her heart was pounding. What should she do? If only Seff were here!

Seff! She had given Seff's things to a Russian. Could she justify helping a man whose comrades Seff might be killing at that very moment? She pressed her hands to her temples. If only she could talk to someone about it! But that would betray him straight away, then the decision would be out of her hands...And what if Seff was captured and, for whatever reason, tried to escape – wouldn't she wish for someone to hide him and give him food? But in any case, Seff was a German. And they didn't go round frenziedly killing unarmed people. Anna heard Mother's steps coming upstairs. She couldn't talk to her now! She lay still as the door opened quietly. Now

Mother was listening. Then the door was closed carefully. Boards creaked.

Now they were eating their evening meal downstairs, unaware that there was a Russian in the barn. If they found him, it would come out that she, Anna, had helped him. They would recognise Seff's clothes, of course. Would they believe what she had thought about mentally disturbed people?

Anna's thoughts went round in circles, looking for ways out. She was hot. Had she got a temperature too?

A Russian. He had waded through the stream to throw off the dogs that might be following his trail. And his pursuers must be furious, now that they hadn't got their hands on him, the last of the eight Ivans. But they had been so close to him: four hundred metres! Human, inhuman . . . And her family were caught up in it too!

She got up and pushed the curtain aside. It had stopped snowing. The sky was cloudless again. Stars shimmered. The snow glistened on the barn roof.

There under the roof lay a Russian: a young man in enemy territory. He had smelled of sweat and dirt when she passed him the milk. No wonder after a flight like that! Did German soldiers on the run smell like that too?

His fate depended on her decision. Probably his life. Such a decision was appalling!

If she hadn't bothered about the footprints, if the man had crawled in somewhere else, if she had pushed down the compulsion to help him, she would not only have been spared all these fears but probably also the scandal that would taint not only her but also her family. After all, it couldn't be hidden for ever, that over there in the hay…

There was a knock on the door.

'Are you asleep?' whispered Felix.

Stupid question. 'Come in,' said Anna. 'And turn the light on.' They blinked at each other. He came in, quite the waiter, balancing a little tray with a cup of lime blossom tea and a plate of sweet dumplings and put it down on the bedside table.

'Are you feeling better?' he asked. 'Because you're supposed to come with us to the Lamb tomorrow.' She didn't answer. 'By the way, the people with the dogs have already left.'

'What?' She caught her breath. 'Why've they gone already?' she asked. 'They haven't caught the last one yet.' He shrugged his shoulders. 'They've searched through all the bunkers. What else should they do? If he hasn't managed to get to the Protectorate, then he's done for anyway. Because he'll either starve or freeze in the forest. And if he's hiding in some barn or other, then sooner or later he'll be found and reported.'

And reported. For Felix it was so obvious. He always just obeyed orders, never questioned what he was taught. For him there were no doubts, everything was good or evil, black or white.

He would be very good looking, you could see that already. At the moment he was still a beanpole, thin and gawky. But that would change. His face was no longer a child's. When she compared him with the pictures in the racial studies chapter in her biology book, his head was of the pure Nordic race. A blond curl bobbed on his forehead. He got that hair from Father. In comparison, Seff, his brother, was dark with straight hair, of medium height, but with wide shoulders. He took after Mother, a Hanisch through and through.

And she herself? Tall and thin like Father, but with dark curls. And Mother's grey eyes. Something from each of them. She glanced at the photo that hung over her bed: Felix Brünner, her father. Parted blond curls, a clean cut face, a narrow moustache, a melancholy smile.

'Nine women from the *Ruhrgebiet* are arriving tomorrow,' she heard Felix say. 'Mothers of the children in the evacuation centre. So the beds need to be made up. First thing in the morning. Because at half past ten it's the memorial for Schroller.'

She jumped up, shocked: 'For Schroller? The one I had in class four? What's happened to him?'

'Killed,' answered Felix. 'What else? In France. Didn't anyone tell you?'

The tears sprang up into her eyes. He had been her favourite teacher.

Felix gave her a sad look and disappeared.

A little later Mother came up again.

'He's sorry to have sprung the news on you like that,' she reported. 'He says, he never guessed that Herr Schroller's death would upset you like that. He never had him as a teacher himself.'

She bent over Anna. 'You look ill. Rings under your eyes. Sleep in tomorrow. I'll ask Grandmother to stand in for you at the Lamb. It'll just be leftovers for lunch though. It's rather tricky because of Hedi. All three children have got whooping cough and the youngest has pneumonia as well. So I can't very well say to her: You've *got* to come . . . !'

And she had gone again. Anna couldn't remember ever having seen her sitting on the edge of her bed.

She felt very alone. Mother: never any time; Seff: gone; Felix: too young; Grandmother: too old; Father: dead.

Father – what would *he* have said about this Russian business? She knew so little about him. Before Felix was even born he had taken his own life, without warning and without leaving a note. She hadn't even been two years old. Apparently he had always conjured sweets out of her nose, sweets from the Grünbaums' shop.

Felix Brünner, Conjuror. He had travelled through the whole of Europe with a circus. He had even been to Moscow several times. 'He often went into raptures about Russia,' Uncle Franz had told her. 'He said that the people there aren't ashamed to bare their souls.'

Anna was always amazed at the way her parents had found each other. Mother had worked as a waitress in Prague long before the beginning of the war. That was where she had met Felix the conjuror when she visited the circus.

'Then I knew: him or nobody!' she had often said. 'When I found out that he was still single, I didn't rest until I had him. That's the way I am. What I want, I get . . .'

Father left the circus and moved with Mother to Stiegnitz, where they married. Mother inherited the inn, but Father didn't become a landlord. He just conjured for the guests now and again, at Mother's request.

Uncle Franz had told her all that on her fourteenth birthday. Mother had asked him to.

Franz and Marie, brother and sister. They got on well. Uncle Franz said he had got on well with Felix Brünner too. Felix just hadn't fitted in to Stiegnitz because he had been so different and had previously lived in such a different world. Her father hadn't been happy in Stiegnitz.

'Why didn't Mother go with him back to the circus then?' Anna had asked her uncle in amazement.

'That would have killed *her*,' he had answered.

And so the inevitable happened.

'Your mother took Felix's death very hard, because she cared for him. So she insisted that the little one was named after him. Felix! What a name!'

Felix would get the Lamb one day, Uncle Franz's farm would go to Seff, and she herself would inherit the little farmstead on which they lived. That had all been arranged already.

Anna had learned once from Grandmother that her father had wanted to name her Eva. The whole Hanisch family had been against it however, because nobody in Stiegnitz or the surrounding villages was called Eva. So Mother had asserted herself with her family: the child was given Grandmother's name. Anna.

Uncle Franz had expressed himself very carefully to her so as not to hurt her: Her father 'hadn't fitted in to Stiegnitz', had been 'so different'. According to Aunt

Agnes, the Hanisch clan had referred to him among themselves as The Eccentric and 'another sort of man'. Aunt Agnes was Uncle Franz's wife so she should know. She also knew that for the local people he had been the Circus guy, the Abracadabra, the crazy man, the lunatic. The one who took in tramps and fed them! Who played cards with gypsies!

Anna knew that it is difficult to be different from others. The people of Stiegnitz were like a flock of sheep. If you stepped out of *their* line, you didn't belong. If Felix Brünner had become a good landlord and spent the evenings telling the latest jokes over a beer, then he would still be alive. Then he would wear the Party badge like Mother and Uncle Franz, and the SA uniform at ceremonies. Or he would be a soldier. Probably on the Eastern Front.

The Eastern Front. So Father had got to know the Russians in their own country and still liked them. He had probably made real friendships there. And he would certainly have met Russian singers and dancers, been in Russian circuses, have got to know the Russian theatre.

How could he, who loved Russia, have shot at Russian soldiers? Probably he would rather have let himself be shot as a conscientious objector.

And *he* hadn't come to terms with the people of Stiegnitz. That was also a fact. That is, he hadn't acted in accordance with the usual principles. What is the done thing here? What will benefit my family and me? Judging by the stories that people told about him, he had, for the most part, spontaneously followed his feelings. Sympathy had played its part there. And tolerance to strangers. And outrage at injustice. He had never lacked the courage to act differently from the villagers when he felt it was necessary. That brought him hatred, damage and even punishment. Yes, he had once actually been locked up for three months because he had helped a Slovakian pedlar to escape from the village prison. The Slovakian had landed up there because he had tried to steal a loaf from the baker's.

The people of Stiegnitz had shaken their heads over Felix Brünner back then: To let himself get a criminal record just for the sake of a lousy Slovakian – incomprehensible! For them, gypsies, tramps, Slovakian pedlars were just riff-raff, to beware of.

Mother had loved Felix Brünner because he was the way he was. That mattered to her. But all the same, she hadn't managed to free herself from the security of the Stiegnitz herd. That was what had killed him.

Anna wasn't just a Hanisch. She was also a Brünner.

She clasped her arms behind her head and stared at the picture of her father. Would he, the lunatic, have betrayed the Russian in the barn? Never!

No, she couldn't do it either. To deliver up a terrified, half-starved man to be shot like an animal – how could she reconcile that with her conscience? She couldn't live with guilt like that, and she didn't want to!

The people with dogs had left the Lamb, left Stiegnitz. That was good. And she, Anna, would be quite alone in the house tomorrow morning. That was good too. The Russian had to get out of the barn – as soon as possible! He must go somewhere where he could recover in peace, and after a couple of days he could go on alone again.

If he and the seven others from Glatz had fled southwards, then doubtless they had intended to reach the Protectorate and disappear among the Czechs.

Russians and Czechs were, so to speak, related, of Slavic origins, and they had something else in common too: Germany was their enemy.

It was about twenty kilometres from Stiegnitz to the border of the Protectorate. That was easy to cover on foot, through the forests. But only if you were healthy. So the Russian had to get back on his feet first. That meant he needed something to eat. Anna would supply him with food.

The stove was roaring. But despite that she was cold, so cold. She heard Felix disappear into the boys' room. Downstairs in Mother's and Grandmother's rooms the noises were stopping too. Now it was totally quiet in the house. She wondered how the Russian was getting on in the hay.

Where should she take him? Just into the forest? He'd freeze. Or someone would find him. Then he'd be sunk. Mother would be certain to know a safe place. It was rare for her not to have any advice, a pat solution. But this problem had greater dimensions than the little aches and pains of the village.

No one else from the family should be dragged into this. She, Anna, would have to make it right alone. But how?

She turned the light off and rolled up under the duvet. She couldn't get warm. By tomorrow morning she had to have thought of a hiding place for the man, somewhere halfway safe. Safe for him – and for her! By tomorrow morning, or she would have missed the chance and everything would be lost.

She tossed and turned, saw what she imagined a prison camp to look like before her eyes, saw police dogs, straining on their leashes, saw tracks in the snow, saw Seff with the lantern in his hands...

Suddenly she sat bolt upright. The bunker! The Moserwald Bunker! That was the answer. They wouldn't be able to find the man so easily in its labyrinth, unless they came with dogs. Inside the mountain it never got very cold either. She would take him there, straightaway in the early morning!

Anna turned the light on again, because suddenly she felt extremely hungry. She drank the tea, which had gone cold by then, and gobbled up five dumplings. And her feet were warm again.

Now she could sleep.

4

Anna was woken by the noises which penetrated from the living room downstairs. Felix's shrill voice couldn't be ignored. Sometimes it dropped. His voice was breaking.

Outside dawn was breaking. She thought about the Russian. What should she give the man so that he would be able to help himself to get further? She planned it all out again.

It was already light when she heard Mother, Grandmother and Felix leave the house. She rushed to get ready. She found two old horse blankets in the loft. They would certainly not be missed. Who needed them now? She also took a rag rug that was beginning to come undone at the edges and a dusty pillow. And Grandfather's boots, which he had worn in the house towards the end. The Russian would need strong footwear – and Grandmother wouldn't notice. A sack was hanging over a rafter. She pulled it down and stuffed it all in.

A spoon too, a kitchen knife. A knife? She considered. A knife was a weapon. Shouldn't she wait till later to . . . ? But then she shook her head and put it in anyway. He would need something to cut with, and in his condition he could hardly attack her. The man should also have a big handled cup, decorated with little flowers, from the second row in Grandmother's kitchen cupboard. After all, it was never used.

Anna packed in more: a big piece of bread, wrapped in paper. Apples, peas and hazel nuts from the cellar. There were plenty of them, and they weren't on coupons. She also added a quarter of the butter pat that was still standing on the table. She was working ever faster, ever more hastily. Because the later she left the farm, the more dangerous it would be.

She looked out and could hardly see the roof of the barn. Fog! She couldn't have wished for anything better...

He would have to live mainly on potatoes out there. She put perhaps fifteen kilos, perhaps even twenty, into a second sack. She found two rusty enamel pans on a cellar shelf along with a lid that, while it didn't belong with them, more or less fitted. She filled a bag with salt and stashed several boxes of matches in a jam jar and screwed on the lid. Three candles would have to go in too.

Hopefully neither Mother nor Grandmother would ever miss it all. Mother was sometimes absent-minded, and Grandmother was often downright forgetful. If necessary a lot could be explained by pointing out these weaknesses. She would only have to be careful of Felix. Because he was neither absent-minded nor forgetful. She would have to think of plausible arguments for him.

While she hastily brewed some tea, despondency rose up in her. How daring this was! It was so dependent on chance! What if Felix came home suddenly! Or some complete stranger walked onto the farm! Or if the fog lifted...

She shivered. She drank some of the tea and put the

rest in a pot, which she took with her, along with the rest of the dumplings.

It was really mild for a December day. It was thawing rapidly. The roofs everywhere were dripping. The tracks in the snow were already half melted or completely disappeared.

She entered the barn, and now, all at once, she was afraid again. A different fear from yesterday evening. What if the man leapt at her from above, stormed into the house, took what he could use and then withdrew into the forest?

But he'd freeze there. He must realise that. After all, he *wasn't* crazy! No, she couldn't back out now. It would go well. Father would have done it too.

With a pounding heart she climbed the stairs.

The Russian received Anna half sitting up. His look betrayed the fact that he was just as afraid of her as she was of him. That made her feel safe. She dared to examine him a bit more closely. It was only now, in daylight, that she realised what an awful state he was in. It wasn't just that his cheeks were so sunken. His eyelids were inflamed, his lips were swollen, his hands covered in wounds. He took some of the food that she gave him and the rest he put away, simply stuffed in his pockets.

He wasn't handsome. His mouth was too wide and his eyebrows almost met over the bridge of his nose. Perhaps the shaved head and reddish stubbly beard made him seem uglier than he was too. And he always pinched his eyes together so.

He was wearing Seff's things now, he had hidden his uniform in the hay. He showed it to her.

It took a while till he grasped that he should go with her. His eyes became suspicious. She showed him the house through a gap in the boards and gestured with her hands – so that he would understand: nobody home.

As he looked over there, he pinched his eyes together again. He nodded – and moved so slowly that she almost despaired. He only got onto his feet and into the boots with a great effort. He had to lean on the wall, he staggered so much. How on earth was she going to get him up the slope? But one thing was sure: he couldn't do anything to her as weak as he was, she would be able to defend herself against him.

She went ahead of him down the stairs and let him wait in the barn until she had fetched the two sacks from the house. In the hallway she grabbed Seff's thick winter cap, the one with the earflaps. That was always hanging there, regardless of whether Seff was at home or not. It was made of fur and leather and had originally come from Grandfather. It would serve to hide the fact that the Russian's head was shaved. Because that could be dangerous. What kind of man would go around like that?

Quick, quick, before it occurred to the fog to flee. The fog was the *one* chance. Everyone kept their eyes on everyone else here, and everyone knew everyone.

Quick, quick! Why didn't the Russian pull the cap over his ears? Yes, the flaps down too, so that the stubble couldn't be seen so easily! And they were off, he with the little sack, she with the big one. How he staggered and sweated! And sometimes he shut his eyes and just stood still.

She was sweating too. This trek to the bunker was the most dangerous part of the business. And the danger of dangers was crossing the bridge. There they were closest to the village. But the fog was so thick, and it was Sunday morning. The people hadn't set out for church yet.

Still, fate could will her to meet some nosy parker, despite the fog. What should she say if she was asked about her companion? And what she was doing herself? For God's sake, what should she say? She hadn't thought of that. A worker from the East who didn't know his way around here? Who had been assigned to a farm in Hossborn, a village in the south? But he'd got lost in the forest and now she was showing him the way there?

Then they would ask after the so-called Eastern worker in Hossborn at the next opportunity. And the two sacks?

Down to the bridge, then up the slope, faster, faster! Her heart was pounding in her throat. If it came out, Uncle Franz couldn't be mayor any more, Mother might have to go to Dachau, Felix would be destroyed, Grandmother would grieve to death. And she and the Russian – what would happen to them?

They met nobody.

Muddy tracks ran along the path which led to the slope. This was where the Russian-catchers and their dogs had tramped through the snow. They must have cursed the Moserwald Bunker on this march. Most of the other bunkers could be reached more comfortably, in off-road vehicles. But here in the woods, the Forestry Authorities had ploughed up a good part of the rubble path, which the Czechs had once laid down for building the bunker, and included it in a plantation area. So if you wanted to go to the Moserwald Bunker, you had to go on foot.

Anna knew the path precisely. She would have found it even if it had been covered in fresh snow and free of tracks. She knew the trees that lined it, the paths that crossed it, the whole landscape around her.

How slowly the Russian walked. He kept stopping, leaning against a tree, wiping the sweat out of his face. Even the potatoes seemed to be too heavy for him. They didn't reach the entrance for a good half hour. If Anna had been alone and had nothing to carry, she would have done the journey in half the time! She glanced quickly into her cell near the entrance. The heather was completely dried out and all that was left of the bed was a pile of straggly branches.

She switched on the torch and led the man through the wide main corridor deeper inside the mountain. They made very slow progress: down here rails had been torn up, bits of old metal were lying around, you could fall over rubble. The beam of the torch fell through the doorways on either side of the corridor into bare, empty rooms.

When the twilight in which they were moving turned into darkness, Anna stood still and gave the sack to the Russian. He bent down to pick it up. As he straightened up again, he stumbled against her.

43

Defensively she raised her hands, took a few quick steps back and turned the torch on his face. He shielded himself from the light with his hands. His gigantic shadow wavered on the wall. He shook his head and said something that she didn't understand. But it sounded as though he wanted to reassure her.

She pointed to Seff's cap. He didn't understand what she wanted, looked around, looked up, shrank back as she took it from his head. How his bald skull shimmered in the light. Now he would be sure to freeze. But she couldn't leave him the hat; Felix would miss it at once. And Grandmother too.

'*Auf wiedersehen*,' she said, although she knew how unsuitable such a greeting was in this situation. He looked at her questioningly, tried to smile. But she only saw a grimace: eye sockets, sunken cheeks, a mouth with teeth missing – and the ugly shaven head.

How dark it was. And there wasn't a sound.

He pointed to her torch. Of course, it seemed reasonable that he should want it. The candles were still in the sack. How could he manage with a candle in his hand, and the bags, and in his condition . . . ?

But give away her torch? She hesitated. What was the danger in not giving it to him? Would he take it from her by force?

He said something and pointed out the entrance, a tiny point of light. He was right, of course: nothing simpler than to walk towards it. But she'd had the torch ever since she'd started at the school in Schonberg! In the winter she badly needed its light on the way to and from

44

the station. And there were hardly any torches to buy now.

There he stood, with an outstretched hand. His mouth was moving; he was saying something else, quietly, hoarsely. She couldn't leave the hand empty. She put the torch into it then turned round and went. There was the speck of light ahead of her.

In front of her was a ghostly shimmer. The man was lighting her way. Now she didn't need to feel her way and stumble. All the iron, the rails, the unevenness of the corridor floor could be seen, cast shadows.

Then she heard steps. Startled, she turned round. Why was he coming after her? Could she be sure that he only wanted to light her way out?

She walked faster.

Then, in the light that came from outside, she began to run and didn't stop until she was under the trees.

The fog was so thick. She could hardly make the Russian out. He was standing there in the bunker entrance and watching after her. He was leaning on the wall. In his miserable condition, he had followed her, to make her way through the tunnel easier! She saw him crouch down and wash his face in the snow.

How much effort it cost him to straighten up again! He shuffled away like an old man, the torch in his hand, and disappeared into the darkness inside the bunker.

Now he would have to get all the way back again!

How quiet it was. Not even the forest was rustling. And how quickly it was thawing! Everywhere it was dripping, running, trickling.

She breathed in deeply and forced the air out again with a loud sigh. Now the whole thing was behind her. In a few days the Russian would leave the bunker, to flee further southwards into the Protectorate. She had done all that she could for him. She didn't know the way into the Czech area. He would have to find that for himself.

He would be bound to try to make it through to there in one of the coming nights. The moon was waxing. And he would keep to the forests.

She ran down the slope in big bounds. An exciting weekend. But it looked as though everything would work out all right. For the Russian and for her, the daughter of the Abracadabra, the other kind of man.

When she was almost at the bridge, she heard distant brass music through the fog, from the direction of the village. She stood still and listened carefully. It was the funeral song 'I had a Comrade'. The memorial for Schroller, the teacher.

Two small girls were turning somersaults on the bridge rails. They hardly looked up as Anna went over. After all, for the last few years she had only lived in Stiegnitz at weekends and in the holidays. Why should the girls know her?

When she arrived back at home, Anna hung the cap back on the hook and glanced into the living room. Then she went over to the barn, climbed up to the loft and piled the hay back up, where the Russian had been lying.

The uniform was still there: tunic, trousers, coat – torn, threadbare, stiff with dirt. She rolled the stuff up together, carried it out and a little way into the forest. She knew of a pile of stones out there. She hid the roll in the middle of it, piled a few stones on it and laid a clump of moss on top. The next snow would cover it all up.

She ran back, wiped snow and mud from her shoes, ran up to her room, peeled off her clothes and crawled into bed.

But she couldn't sleep.

5

'How on earth can you scoff so much?' Grandmother wondered at lunchtime. 'You've already had a good breakfast. Such a lot of butter, and so much bread...'

Anna realised that she was blushing. She lowered her head and blew her nose hastily, then she turned to Felix. He was in uniform. So he wasn't slouching hunched over his plate as he usually did but rather sitting up as straight as a poker. He told her about the memorial: 'Packed out. And a lot of wailing. Uncle Franz gave a good speech, by the way. That Schroller followed the *Führer* and faithfully laid down his life for him, according to the oath of allegiance.'

'Schroller got on so well with the children,' Grandmother said. 'Such a pity.' She cleared her throat. 'Such pointless bloodshed. None of those people have anything against each other. Not even the soldiers. If there was peace, and Germans and French were together, they'd sit down together in the inn. And the Russians too.'

'Rubbish!' shouted Felix heatedly. 'The Russians aren't such valuable people as we are. They're hardly a proper race at all. Anyway, we need their land. There are nearly a hundred million of us. There isn't enough room here!'

'You're even better than Goebbels,' said Anna mockingly.

'Stop grinning like that!' Felix turned on her. 'You've learnt that in school too!'

'Yes,' sighed Grandmother, 'you learn stuff like that in school now. But taking land away is unjust, whatever scale it's on, and however you dress it up. It's in the Bible!'

Anna was of the same opinion, even if she didn't share her Grandmother's religious views. Grandmother was seventy-one already and she couldn't adjust to the new times. She held fast to her little family altar with the brass crucifix and the tacky Sacred Heart painting. She had defended the living room fiercely when Mother had wanted to put a picture of Hitler on the shelf in the corner. 'Stick your Hitler where you like!' she had said furiously. 'But not here in the living room!'

'He's seen to it that you get a pension!' Mother had shouted at her. Mother could really shout when she got angry.

So Grandmother had given in, but full of resentment. 'Well not in God's corner then. You can put it on the chest of drawers with the mirror over there if you like.'

That was the wall that was furthest from the crucifix. But in any case, he, Hitler, was in the living room now, much to Mother's satisfaction. She, as landlady, tried to be on good terms with *everyone*. She was very good at that, just like Uncle Franz. They got on splendidly with the district leaders and local group leaders in the area, the SA and SS men with authority, the people from the army and policemen of all ranks, whenever they had to deal with them.

But they also tried to win the trust of the few Czechs who lived in Stiegnitz. Times change. You never know... Mother and Grandmother used to be on very friendly terms with the Jewish Grünbaums. They didn't like to remember that now though. But there was hardly anything left to remember them by. All the Jews were long gone, and nobody asked the question: Where are they now?

'Have either of you seen the flowery cup?' asked Grandmother.

Anna jumped. 'I took it to Schonberg with me,' she said, deliberately casually. 'Because I broke one of the Beraneks' cups.'

'You could at least have asked,' said Grandmother reproachfully. Shaking her head, she added: 'I could have sworn that I saw it in the cupboard only this morning.'

'Yes, yes, you're getting old...' sighed Felix mischievously.

'You've spilled something down you,' countered Grandmother dryly. 'Right in the middle of your manly chest.'

She knew how to handle him. Shocked he jumped up. She wiped away the spot with hot water. And he already had to leave, for a Hitler Youth meeting in the next village. He never missed anything. After all, he was supposed to get his *Führer*'s stripe soon. Being a *Führer* was his dream.

He came back punctually from his meeting to accompany Anna part of the way to the station. Grandmother

50

insisted on it, 'because of the Russian'. After all, that one was still running about the place. Felix didn't resist. When Anna complained that she had lost her torch, he helped her out with his own. She was welcome to keep it till the next weekend. Mother had another replacement lamp.

He could be like *that* too. He insisted on carrying her bags and promised her a great Christmas present. From him personally.

What did he want from her? He had no need to consider.

'Target sheets,' he said. 'A whole load. I want to be a good shot *before* I become a soldier. I'm getting an air rifle from Mother, she's promised it to me. She's buying it from a woman. It belonged to her son, but he was killed.'

'Target sheets. So long as it's nothing else,' exclaimed Anna, laughing.

Once he had wanted a large map of Europe from her, complete with pins and little flags which he wanted to mark the frontlines with. The map had hung in the living room for a long time, until the point when the German victories were over and the fronts were shrinking back to Germany. Then he had let it disappear, and Anna knew where it was too: folded up in the top drawer of the chest with the mirror, under Grandmother's sewing things.

Even now there was no reason to get it out again. On the contrary. The news was getting ever more gloomy. Anna wasn't keen on knowing exactly where the Russians, English and Americans had got to. Bomb victims were lodging in Stiegnitz and Schonberg, and she didn't like to

51

hear them describing the way things looked in Hamburg and Hanover now. But one thing was clear: the fronts were shrinking ever closer to Germany. In the West – and in the East.

She was suddenly struck by a vague feeling that the future progress of the war could have a lot to do with her and the fate of the Russian. But she quickly thought of something else.

They passed the point where on the day before Anna had noticed the Russian's tracks. But now all you could see there were unclear impressions in the snow. Nothing to pose a puzzle or feed suspicions.

In her thoughts Anna could see the bunker. The man up there would have been sure to have sought out a room lying deep inside the mountain by now. Now he would be sitting on the rag rug, wrapped in the horse blanket and staring into the candlelight...

Felix had only wanted to accompany her halfway. But in the end he walked all the way to the station. When he wandered away into the darkness she waved after him, touched. He was all right really, if a bit hard to take at the moment – now he was at the most difficult age.

Felix turned round once more and called: 'Perhaps he'll run into my arms on the way home!'

'Who?' asked Anna, puzzled.

'Well the Russian of course!' He raised his arms and shouted boisterously: 'I'm off, wish me happy hunting!'

It was a week like any other. That was, as the last few weeks had been. Since the end of the summer holidays the girls' school building had been used as a hospital. So lessons were taking place in the boys' school: in the hall, the gym, in the cellar, yes even in the map room. And then there were piano lessons – and of course the League service: evening meetings on Wednesdays, sport on Saturdays. And homework, which Anna always did very thoroughly.

Sometimes she went to the Café Paris with school friends, sometimes to the cinema. She was occasionally invited to the cinema by Frau Beranek too, because she didn't like to go on her own. After some films she let observations fall, which would have enraged Felix, if he had heard them. And they were probably enough to transport Frau Beranek to Dachau, just like the ten little grumblers. Frau Beranek disliked it above all when everything was so black and white, like in the film *Jud Süss*: here are the good Aryans, there are the bad Jews. Or in *Ohm Krüger*: here are the noble Boers, there are the evil British. After visiting the cinema she could let off steam about that sort of thing until late at night, when Anna would have rather been reading. Because she read passionately.

Until recently one of her favourite authors had been Edwin Erich Dwinger. Until Frau Beranek had put her off him. Anna had particularly liked *Army behind Barbed Wire* and *Between White and Red*. They were books that wouldn't let you sleep after reading them, books that hadn't been written for young girls. But then she was nearly sixteen, and the current situation had little in common with the worlds of children's books. Now even fifteen-year-olds were taken seriously. In the *Volkssturm* for example. And the flak auxiliaries weren't much older. And she too would probably have to take the place of radio operators and telephonists as an air force or intelligence auxiliary, even before she had finished school. No seventeen-year-olds fell in action in books for little girls; no children were burnt to a cinder in the bombing. However, with Dwinger there were streams of blood, festering wounds and death was not only heroic, but also hideous. For example an Army officer was beaten up in Berlin, and when he was already down on the floor, they kicked his monocle into his eye too. And who were these monsters? The Communists. It was like that in all Dwinger's books: all evil came out of the East. From the Left. From the Reds, the Communists, the Bolsheviks. They were all murderers. And mostly it was beastly. Even Anna's favourite hero, the very young Lieutenant Willmuth, fell victim to them.

But Frau Beranek had objected that all the good was never on one side, nor all the evil on the other. Not even now. She was of the opinion that 'Next to the good in every individual, there is also evil'.

There was something in that. Anna could see it in herself. Sometimes she thought that she was a good person, but sometimes she was horrified at herself. Felix too was such a mixture. And Grandmother. And Mother. And Hitler.

She had got to know a Bolshevik. He had acted like a perfectly normal person, had even thanked her! How would he act as a conqueror? Was he an exception, when you thought about the events of Nemmersdorf? Could Frau Beranek's opinion be applied to the Russians too? Were they good and evil in one as well? Then Dwinger, then the German propaganda, would be wrong...

That week, all this came into Anna's thoughts more frequently than usual. What was right? What was wrong?

On the way home towards the end of the school week, she found herself, as so often, thinking about *her* Russian again. He was bound to have left the bunker by now. Or was he? Anna started suddenly. She hadn't thought of that. Perhaps he didn't know where he was at all and was still in his hiding place! She reproved herself for not having given him a map.

And what if he had still tried to go on? Wandering around in Seff's things and Grandfather's boots! Near the village!

She felt dizzy. But what could she do from here, from Schonberg? Nothing. She would have to wait until the next weekend. It would just have to be all right. It had to be!

Anna tried to push down her worries with Christmas shopping. It was the week before the second Sunday of Advent. So close to the festival there was more going on in the shops than usual. There were even dolls at Matzels on Adolf-Hitler-Strasse. Women were queuing right out into the street. Anna scoured all the shops and found a vase for Mother and wooden eggcups for Grandmother. On Bahnhofstrasse she got hold of a whole packet of target sheets for Felix. Searching for a present for Frau Beranek, she happened on an ironmonger's where she discovered a torch complete with batteries. The last one! What luck.

But she still hadn't got anything for Frau Beranek. The only things available in any number were hand-crafted items: wooden fairy tale figures for children's rooms, embroidered pin cushions, framed water colours, turned wooden cups from the Erzgebirge and suchlike. And of course books, with Hitler resplendent on the cover. Or the swastika. Or a soldier's face under a steel helmet. That was all out of the question.

In the end she decided on a little box, which turned out to be a jack-in-the-box when you opened the lid. The whole thing was small enough to fit into one hand. A joke. Better than nothing.

She waded through the slush. Her shoes weren't watertight any more. In the light from the blacked-out lanterns you could hardly see what you were treading in anyway. Christmas spirit? Not that you'd notice. And grief reigned in so many households.

As Anna came back to her attic room with wet feet, a plate of Christmas biscuits was standing there. How nice of Frau Beranek! Especially as she had neither hens, nor a goat, nor an Uncle Franz as a black market butcher. She just lived on what she could get on the coupons and from a little kitchen garden behind the house. Anna ran downstairs to thank her.

She told her about the torch. Such a piece of luck: the last one! She didn't have her old one any more you see, she'd given it to a—

She stopped abruptly, shocked. But Frau Beranek didn't dig any deeper. She seemed to have her mind on something else.

'What do you actually think of the Russians?' asked Anna.

Frau Beranek began to laugh. 'From the torch to the Russians!' she cried. 'I'd like to be able to read your thoughts!' Then she became serious again and said quietly: 'Well, if you ask *me* – I am of the opinion that they are no better and no worse than we are. So long as they aren't inflamed by their rabble-rousers.' She bent down to Anna and whispered: 'We shouldn't let ourselves be stirred up by rabble-rousers either!'

To say something like that was dangerous. But that was Frau Beranek: she said what she thought. Anna liked her.

Two days later when Anna came home from the school canteen she heard her landlady crying loudly. She learned from a neighbour that Herr Beranek had been killed. Anna had known him too. After all, he had come home on leave sometimes. A tall, thin man with glasses, a joker ... partner of Bartel the optician.

On that evening Anna couldn't do her homework. She heard Frau Beranek crying downstairs and thought about Seff. If one day he ...? She wrote a long letter to him and wrapped it in a military post parcel.

And tomorrow – tomorrow was Saturday. Going home. What would have happened in Stiegnitz?

6

Nothing. It was all quiet. Nobody said anything about the Russian.

Anna was just about to breathe out in relief when Grandmother went up into the attic and discovered that the sack was no longer hanging from its rafter. When she started looking for it, she soon missed the two horse blankets and Grandfather's boots as well. She got utterly confused and suspected Felix of having taken the things for himself, for some reason or other. But he hadn't even known that the blankets existed and radiated innocence.

Anna's references to Grandmother's poor memory had no effect. Mother had seen the things in the attic too. She puzzled about it while she hastily pulled on her coat. A burglar in Stiegnitz? Impossible. After all everyone knew everyone else here! And she already had to go out again. They would consider what to do about it later. But until then, please keep quiet! Felix had to leave again too, in uniform of course. He advised Grandmother to wait a bit. It was bound to turn up again!

But Grandmother didn't want to wait. Grandfather's boots were sacred! She grabbed her headscarf and was about to set straight off for Uncle Franz. He would take the matter in hand...

Anna was shocked. If she didn't manage to head Grandmother off, then before long the whole village would be talking about the missing blankets, boots and sack. She would tell everybody she met. And then if the Russian really hadn't left, if he was still hiding in the bunker and someone found him there? And the lost things with him! Then she, Anna, would be for it – as someone who helped Russians! As a traitor! And the whole family would be dragged in with her!

Careful not to show her agitation, she persuaded Grandmother to leave it to her to talk to Uncle Franz, and set out at once. She was so flustered that she put her hat on inside out. Grandmother took it off her head and turned it round for her. Hardly had Anna left the house than she was gasping for air. Now what? What she had done *mustn't* come out!

Mother. She would take Mother into her confidence; tell her the whole thing, the truth. She would soon make everything right, with or without Uncle Franz's help. The main thing was that she would explain things to Grandmother in such a way that her gossip couldn't do any harm.

Into the Lamb! A Father Christmas plodded by, a couple of cherubs trembled in the draught from the hallway. A Christmas carol sounded from the function room. Hedi hurried past Anna in a frilly white apron, her face bright red, Mother's best worker and general dogsbody. She hardly had time to say hello to Anna.

And then Mother came out of the function room, just as red-faced, shouted something to Hedi and whispered, before Anna had even had a chance to speak to her: 'No time, no time! We'll talk about it all later at home.'

Later at home, that meant at twelve or one. At the earliest. Then Mother would be ready to drop and not in a state to talk calmly about something so important.

So, go to Uncle Franz after all? He was a sly fox as she'd heard people say. In fact, he'd got into scrapes a couple of times and had always found a way out. When they caught him illegally slaughtering a pig for example, and confiscated the sow, he'd just called the District Nazi Party leader. They were on first name terms, and every year the Christmas goose on his family's dinner table came from Uncle Franz, as did their Christmas tree. The party leader had then got on to the senior inspectors, had declared the unreported slaughter to be an 'urgent special order within the remit of Party conference, on the highest authority' and dropped proceedings against the mayor of Stiegnitz. In return, Uncle Franz had given him a quarter of the pig. That wasn't a bit too much. Because you could get a couple of months in prison for that. After all, someone who kept a whole pig for himself instead of sharing it with his National Comrades was 'an enemy of the people'.

And he had even wangled the business with Wenzel Krause in his own way. Wenzel had been forcibly taken to the Institution in Sternberg. But his mother had kept on badgering Uncle Franz, she wanted her son back, he wouldn't hurt a fly and wouldn't do nearly so well anywhere apart from at home. And so Uncle Franz had sent off a petition: Herr Wenzel Krause was indispensable to the community of Stiegnitz, he cut wood for all the women whose husbands were at the Front and took on other such physical tasks which couldn't be expected of women. He was practically irreplaceable. And so Wenzel Krause came home again, and his mother swore her undying gratitude to Uncle Franz.

Anna only met Aunt Agnes. She was baking cakes. Uncle Franz was in the barn with Kora who had just had four puppies.

The large, fat man with the Hitler moustache under his nose was bending over an old zinc basin. Inside it lay Kora with her puppies. He lifted one of the males out and laid him in Anna's hand. How warm the little creature was!

'Felix will be surprised,' said Uncle Franz.

But Anna didn't want to talk to him about puppies or about Felix either. Time was pressing. She had to make him stop Grandmother quickly.

She stroked the puppy and laid it back with its mother in the basin. Then she turned to Uncle Franz.

'Have you heard any news about the Russian recently?' she asked, as if in passing, and tried to suppress the tremble in her voice.

Uncle Franz didn't grasp straight away who she meant. Oh yes, *that* Russian. No, not yet. All the bunkers had been combed a good week ago. With dogs. Nothing. It was as if the last of the eight had disappeared off the face of the earth. He'd probably managed to get into the Czech area and disappear. In that case the fellow'd been very lucky. If they'd caught him, they'd have made short work of him.

'Do you really think he'd have been shot, even if he

gave himself up?' Anna asked her uncle. She looked at him in consternation.

'Not an Englishman, Frenchman or American,' said Uncle Franz, fondling Kora. 'But a Russian life isn't worth very much for those who have the say at the moment. Bang – problem solved. The main thing is that by implementing that procedure they save themselves the expense of transporting him back,' he added sarcastically.

It took Anna's breath away.

'But if you could decide what to do with the Russian just on your own,' she said, 'would you let him live?'

'Let's talk about something else!' answered Uncle Franz roughly. 'Everything has ears here: the wall, the wind, even the woods. But ask yourself this: Would you risk your life for the sake of a Russian prisoner? Because if you help an Ivan and get caught, you've had it.'

Now Anna had had enough. She had another look at the puppies in the basin and said goodbye.

'Did you want anything in particular?' asked Uncle Franz.

No, she'd been passing and had just popped in.

'Tell Felix he can come and look at the whelps!'

With her lips pressed tightly together Anna walked home through the village. She had wanted help but instead Uncle Franz had, once again, made her drastically aware of the danger she was in. And she couldn't go back because she hadn't reported the Russian at once. Above all it had once more been made clear to her that she must involve neither Mother nor

Uncle Franz if she didn't want to bring them into great danger as well. What had she let herself in for? She hoped fervently that the Russian had already gone. And Grandmother? Anna would have to find a way out on her own. She would have to get Grandmother to keep quiet. And she'd have to do it at once!

She had an idea. She would have to put on an act and swallow her pride. And so, almost as soon as she had arrived home, she sat down next to Grandmother and, crying, confessed to her: she had taken the things herself for a play at the League. She had needed boots, blankets and a sack. But on the next afternoon when she had wanted to collect the props, they had all disappeared. And she hadn't dared to tell them at home.

'But why didn't you just ask us if you could take the things with you to Schonberg?' cried Grandmother and, touched, pulled Anna close.

'I was afraid you wouldn't let me,' sobbed Anna. 'But I'm sorry!'

Grandmother forgave her. Now the story wouldn't be all round the village. All that Anna needed now, however, was to be sure. Was the Russian still in his hiding place? If he had gone, she didn't need to worry so much. If he was still up there in the bunker, she would have to help him to get further away.

She crawled into bed and brooded.

Sunday morning was cold and clear. Grandmother went to the early mass, Mother to the Lamb, Felix to see Uncle Franz.

Anna seized the opportunity and hurried up to the bunker. She dragged her sledge behind her. That way there would be a reason for her walk if she bumped into someone.

Was he still in the bunker or had he gone? Her heart was pounding.

The entrance yawned as black as ever. She left the sledge behind, took the new torch out of her pocket and entered the corridor. In passing she glanced into the first room, her summer 'hermitage'.

She couldn't believe her eyes. There he lay, on the pile of twigs that had once been her bed, the Russian! He had covered himself with both blankets, but they weren't long enough. Anna could see his feet in Grandfather's boots, and underneath, the rag rug.

She approached him cautiously. By his head, on the floor, lay Grandmother's flowered cup, half full of water. Probably melted snow. Next to that was the torch.

She bent over him. His eyes were shut. He had wrapped the empty potato sack around his head, round his forehead and cheeks as well. His face lay in shadow. You could think it was a woman lying there.

Why in all the world had he chosen this room which everyone would look in if they ventured inside the bunker? Surely he must have realised that almost all the other rooms were safer than this one!

She cleared her throat. He didn't move. He seemed to be very fast asleep.

Maybe he'd given up? Was he now indifferent to whether he lived or died? Was he now prepared to let someone find him because he could see no way out? Or was he so ill that he didn't know what he was doing any longer?

Then she had a horrible thought. The man was already dead. This was a corpse!

It gave her the creeps. She had never seen a dead body. Not even her grandfather, who'd died in hospital. She backed out of the room without letting the reclining figure out of her sight.

Hardly was she out into the corridor, than she made a dash for the fresh air, grabbed the string on the sledge and hurried down the slope.

She stayed in her room until she left in the late afternoon. Grandmother and Felix were helping Mother in the Lamb. So nobody could see how upset Anna was.

Oh Father, dear Father, she thought. Do some magic for me. Let me think about something else apart from him up in the bunker. Show me all your tricks. And help me!

She stood in front of the big mirror and stared at herself. She saw a girl with tousled dark curls, big eyes, pale face. Her lips were similar to her father's.

She looked herself in the eyes. Would she stand there like that if they condemned her to death?

Doors banged downstairs. The others were coming home. Anna stared at her reflection and threw back her head.

Anna only left her room and said her goodbyes when it was time to leave for the station. Grandmother carried a big bag with sandwiches, sausage and boiled eggs right out into the hall after her, which she reluctantly stashed in her luggage. In the process she came on Felix's torch. She gave it to Grandmother. It belonged to Felix, he had lent it to her.

'And give my regards to Frau Beranek!' Grandmother called after her. As always.

Oh yes, in all that she had been through that weekend, Anna had completely forgotten to tell them.

'Herr Beranek was killed,' she called back and heard Grandmother's appalled exclamation: 'Holy Mary, Mother of God!'

7

It was a dreadful week. On the following Saturday Anna could no longer remember how she had got through it.

The Beraneks' house was in a state of suppressed bustle. People came and went with sad faces; Frau Beranek's eyes were red with crying. Anna crept up and down the stairs on tiptoe. In the brief periods when she stayed in her cold attic, she spent the time in bed, staring at the ceiling. She saw the Russian lying motionless.

She felt that she was beginning to understand more clearly, that in the condition he'd been in, he'd been unable to do more than to get from the entrance to that room.

What a death. After all, he'd already been very ill when she'd led him to the bunker. What must it be like to know that you would soon die? Did Seff sometimes think about the fact that he might not have long to live? Did somebody who knew he was going to his death see the world through different eyes?

Once she dreamt that the Russian sat up and looked at her piercingly. And then he smiled. She saw the gaps in his teeth quite clearly. She began to feel so light, so light: he was alive!

But when she woke up, the fear was back. What if someone found him! It would immediately unleash all sorts of investigations and questioning. Uncle Franz had said once: They have ways of finding everything out.

From everyone. She realised she would have to go to the bunker again, have to fetch everything out that could give them clues as to who had helped the Russian. But in the room where he lay, it must be ice cold. The corpse must be frozen through and through. How could she get the boots off the feet, the clothes off the body...?

She didn't dare to think any further about it.

She made a bad impression at school several times that week. Once it was because she hadn't done her maths homework. Another time she completely failed to notice that the geography teacher had asked her a question. And then there was the business of the chemistry test. Anna sat with her head in her hands and didn't write anything. When the teacher asked her why she wasn't writing, she answered that her head ached so badly that she couldn't think straight. The teacher, an old man who would have retired long ago in peacetime, sent her home and entered her as ill in the register.

The next day she appeared at school again. Someone asked her why she was so pale. She hardly joined in the conversations of her classmates, and if anyone spoke to her, her answers were distracted and absent-minded.

Only once did she wake up fully: when the rumour started running around the class that Jili, a young Czech waiter from the Café Paris, had been summarily executed. He had belonged to an underground organisation.

Anna too had known and liked him. He had been young and good looking, blond hair, blue eyes and always friendly. But still, a Czech.

'How do you know that?' she asked.

'Don't you ever listen to the radio at six in the morning?' the girl sitting next to her asked in return. 'That's when they always read out the names of the Czechs they've executed. Some for spying and others because they were partisans.'

'Women too?' asked Anna.

'There's no difference there,' came the answer.

A new reason to brood. Of course, it was the same for women as for men. But without a trial, without being able to defend yourself, without the chance to explain why you'd done it – was that right? Could you just stand before the firing squad or under the gallows and scream, 'It was out of pity, out of pity, out of pity!'?

She didn't go to the cinema with the other girls, or to the Café Paris, declined a birthday invitation, turned up for her piano lesson without practising. She hardly spoke during the Wednesday League meeting and excused herself in advance from the sports on Saturday: she had her period. Almost as soon as she had the last lesson of the week behind her, she raced to the station and left for home two hours earlier than usual. But she wouldn't turn up at home two hours early! Oh, if only today were already over!

When she got off in Mellersdorf, the sun was shining, the snow glistening. In front of the station children were sliding about noisily on frozen puddles. A soldier whistled after Anna. She didn't turn round but strode on faster. She wanted to get what she had to do behind her

69

as soon as possible. She had wrapped an old scarf around her neck, one that she couldn't stand. Later on she would throw it in a bin somewhere in Schonberg.

She dreaded it.

She reached the other bank of the stream over the footbridge and walked on down a wide path. Every puddle was frozen, the snow packed hard. She took the side path up to the Moserwald Bunker. She slipped a couple of times, but even so she walked ever faster. Just half an hour after arriving in Mellersdorf, she came to the crossing which led to the bunker entrance. She looked ahead carefully. There were no fresh prints on the path; she could hardly even make out her own from the previous weekend.

Before going closer to the dark rectangle she looked round once more. Nobody for miles around. Only crows cawing, a woodpecker hammering. Down in the valley the roofs of Stiegnitz glistened. It couldn't have been any more peaceful.

She took a deep breath as she plunged into the darkness of the bunker. He was lying in there, dead and stiff. She would peel him out of the blankets and sack, put the scarf under his shoulders and pull him down from the pile of twigs, out of the room, through the long, long main corridor over the rails and rubble, into a far distant and hidden room somewhere, where they would be unlikely to find him. There, deep inside the mountain, there was no frost. In a week she would be able to take the clothes off his body.

She felt ill, just from thinking about it. But only then,

when he was no longer wearing Seff's clothes and Grandfather's boots, would she be free from fear.

She put down her two bags inside, just next to the entrance. Her heart was hammering as she crept to the door of the cell.

The room was empty! No corpse, no blankets – nothing. Only a potato, among the twigs which made up the bed. So they had found him and taken him away, probably down to Stiegnitz. She went cold from shock.

She almost forgot to take her bags with her. She also forgot that she must only arrive home at the usual time. She wanted to know right away whether he had been found. Mother and Uncle Franz must surely be in great difficulties already.

And what would happen to *her*?

She shivered.

It was only when she was deep in the woods on the slope that she suddenly stopped, turned around and looked uphill. Had they really taken him to Stiegnitz? How did you get a body down into the valley in winter? On a sledge of course. But she hadn't seen fresh prints, either from shoes, or from a sledge, on the path to the bunker or anywhere else. Only birds had hopped through the snow, and over there, a rabbit.

She tried to remember. No, it hadn't snowed all last week, and it had hardly thawed. And the sun had only been out for an hour, two at the most. If someone had found the Russian and taken him down to the village, then there would be a broad pattern of prints to be seen. And not just here, up there at the bunker entrance too.

But there was nothing there apart from her own footmarks. Not even the trail of a solitary man, out of the bunker and into the forest to the south, towards the Protectorate.

So the Russian must still be in the bunker. And alive, at that.

Anna turned round, tramped up the slope again as quickly as she could and rushed into the bunker. She took the torch and set off. Carefully she lit up the floor around her feet. She mustn't stumble, mustn't fall. Because nobody would look for her here if she injured herself badly.

She picked up a stone and occasionally banged it twice on the wall as she walked. It echoed. If the Russian was hiding somewhere in one of the rooms, he would definitely hear the sound of knocking. She was getting deeper and deeper inside the mountain. Once she turned off the light and stood in total darkness. Hastily, she switched the torch on again. Desperately she fought against the fear that was rising up in her. Go on! Should she make her presence known? A Hello! would be harmless. It let you call, even if you didn't want others to hear more than an echo.

It smelt musty. It wasn't nearly as cold here as outside. The passage was bending a bit. It seemed to her to be getting lighter. Indeed, it was brighter; she could make out the torch.

The passage ended abruptly by a narrow shaft which fell vertically into the depths, so that you couldn't tell whether or not it was full of water. To the side, a narrow metal staircase ascended to a circular section of sky, stopping at the edge of the shaft. It shimmered in the sun, the top torn off. There must have been one of the huge gun towers revolving up there once.

She had never ventured this far before. She picked up a pebble and threw it down the shaft. After a few seconds she heard it splash.

Was it a well? Or a ladder shaft which led down to deeper levels and was now full of rainwater? How alone she was here. Even her breath seemed to have an echo. Puzzling. Where on earth was the Russian? She couldn't possibly search through all the side passages of this labyrinth. What should she do? Indecisively she stumbled back to the corridor.

Then suddenly something shone a couple of metres ahead of her. She jumped. Her pulse began to race. She turned the torch on the person opposite her – whoever it might be. And then she-recognised him from Seff's loden jacket. He leant against the wall and said hoarsely: 'Hello.'

Anna felt completely relieved. Everything else would sort itself out somehow. Hesitantly she went towards him.

She noticed that his hair had grown. And the stubble had become a proper beard. His eyes seemed to lie even deeper in their sockets. He beamed at her. Obviously he was relieved too.

It must have been like this. After the fever and deep sleep in which she had seen him last Sunday, he had become strong enough to withdraw deeper inside the bunker.

He indicated the door opening next to him, made signs to her to follow him and lurched ahead of her through several pitch-black rooms. After crossing a narrow corridor, they reached a room which was lit by daylight from above. Broken slabs of concrete lay around. Roots hung down some distance from the edge of the hole in the roof. The floor under the hole was wet; some of the roots were dripping. The flowered cup stood under the most prolific of these.

The Russian shone the torch into a dark adjacent room. There in a corner lay the rug, the blankets and the pillow. He also led Anna into another room which was as big as a hall. Here too, the twilight stemmed from a blast hole in the ceiling. A thin stream of water ran down from one rim of this hole straight into the enamel pot. It was half full. Melt-water.

She looked around. The floor of this room was obviously not level, because half of it was covered with water. It seemed to be about a hand span deep on the opposite wall. So there was no shortage of water here.

But where was a place for a fire? After all, the man couldn't eat the potatoes raw. And he would have to warm himself. She sniffed. It didn't smell of smoke. She made a movement as if striking a match and pointed at a piece of wood lying in a corner. He understood and shook his head. He mimed smoke and indicated his eyes. Yes, he was right. A column of smoke coming out of the bunker would be noticed, however thin it was. And the firelight would hide dangers. The Russian shook his head again. He didn't seem to want to take any risks.

So he must have eaten the potatoes raw.

Anna glanced at her watch. She would have to hurry, if she didn't want to cause any worry at home. But there was still the matter of Seff's clothes, the blankets, Grandfather's boots, the sack. She couldn't take all that away from him without bringing replacements. He'd freeze. A new problem, which at that moment seemed insoluble. But she would have to come up with new clothes for him. And quickly, so he would be able to leave the bunker...

At least she could take care of more provisions for him. He probably had nothing left to eat apart from the few potatoes and carrots that she had seen lying next to the rag rug.

And she would bring a calendar, so she could show him when she would come back. Because that was hard to explain with gestures. There was still an old calendar in her room, which she didn't need: on the front January to June and on the back July to December. And all the Sundays in red. He would understand the system, even if he couldn't read the German words.

This time he only went with her as far as the main corridor – probably in order to save his strength. She drew an unobtrusive cross next to the opening in the corridor with a stone and put a rusty pipe from a pile of rubble crossways underneath it. That way, she'd know the place again.

Once again in farewell, he had said the word that must mean 'thank you'. It had sounded like '*spassibo*'.

How polite he had been. In the rooms he had lit the

floor by her feet so that she didn't stumble over the rubble. He had been so happy to see her. And he hadn't attacked her.

8

She was slightly late when she arrived home, panting and out of breath. Only Grandmother was in. She was glad to see Anna happy again after the last few miserable weekends. And she could also give her some good news: Seff had written!

There were already three candles burning on the advent wreath, although it was only Saturday. And once again, something in the oven smelled good. This time it was a ring cake. But before that there was liver dumpling soup. Anna ate very slowly. However, as soon as Grandmother had disappeared to milk the goats, she carried a plate piled with pieces of cake up to her room, grabbed her rucksack, rushed into the cellar, threw in winter apples and a couple of handfuls of prunes and sliced dried pears – Grandmother surely wouldn't have counted them – and bent over the potato crate. But raw potatoes? No. Only animals ate raw potatoes.

Her eye fell on a big pan full of *Blutwurst*. So Uncle Franz had slaughtered another pig. Probably illegally. Quickly, a sausage in the rucksack too, and upstairs again! By the time Grandmother came back from the shed, Anna had been back at the table for a while, the empty plate in front of her, reading Seff's letter.

There wasn't a lot in it. He was well; he'd had a lot of luck lately. He hoped to see them all again in the new year. Mother shouldn't work too hard. How was Anna doing at school? And how tall was Felix now? He should try to get older as slowly as possible...

Felix wouldn't have liked reading that. Nor that: 'It looks as if I'll soon be closer to you.' What Seff meant by that was easy to understand. Retreat on all fronts. After all, thousands of refugees were already streaming westwards out of Memelland, the Warthegau and the eastern part of East Prussia. And the British and Americans were advancing in the west, had long ago crossed the German border. How on earth could they make a Final Victory from all that? Why wasn't Hitler doing anything?

'As long as the boy just comes home healthy,' sighed Grandmother. 'I fear the worst...'

'Grandmother!' cried Anna, shocked. 'What are you saying?'

Grandmother mumbled something into the stove. The hairclips over her ears gleamed; a hairpin had half slipped from her bun. Her hair was so white and her back so crooked, poor Grandmother. What a life she'd had. Always working. And now the war and the fear for her grandson.

'You just can't believe it,' said Grandmother loudly. 'A whole nation lets itself be led by such a godless man. Who doesn't eat meat. Who never goes to church. Who has put such a spell on the people that they believe more in him than in the Almighty. Just talking about God occasionally won't bring in the harvest...'

That was the sort of thing Grandmother noticed:

Hitler occasionally mentioned the Lord God. But it seemed that there was something she *wanted* to forget.

Exactly where the lovage and lemon balm shrubs in the garden came from, for example. In any case, she never talked about it. She had retrieved them from a neighbouring garden on a foggy day in '38, just after the Germans marched into Stiegnitz. From the Grünbaums' garden. They had just been in time to flee from the Germans. Anna had found that out from another girl from Stiegnitz at school who'd been walking by the fence and recognised Grandmother, despite the head-scarf pulled down over her face.

Had Grandmother mentioned that at confession?

Felix came home and filled the living room with noise. He brought big news with him. A big offensive had begun in the Ardennes. He was celebrating: 'Now we'll drive them out! In a few days there won't be any more Western Front. That'll take the wind out of the Russians' sails too!'

Anna let him bluster, helped Grandmother with the washing up and then went up to her room. She had other things to think about.

No, the fear for herself and her family hadn't been banished since that afternoon. It was just pushed a bit further into the background. The pressure of fear would only be relieved when there was no longer anything in the bunker, which could betray where it had come from.

She would have to be very careful. Think everything through. No longer act according to the principle that everything would work out somehow. Be ever alert. Be ever suspicious. And think carefully before she spoke.

That meant that from today, she would have to act like an adult.

Early on Sunday morning she went with them to the Lamb and helped out there. Mother was pleased with her. But Anna only stayed until ten and then left, though not before stashing a couple of stale rolls and a jar of dripping in her coat. The fat came from Uncle Franz's home butchering too, and she was fairly certain that Mother didn't know how many jars of iron rations she had there in the stores. She also slipped in half a dozen tallow candles. Candles didn't burn as brightly as a wood fire and at least you could warm your hands on them.

Grandmother was at church when she got home and there was no sign of Felix either. He was probably at the Hitler Youth as on most Sunday mornings. She emptied her coat pockets, fetched another slice of bread out of the living room and stuffed it all in her rucksack. The Russian wouldn't starve whatever else happened.

But how on earth could she get hold of unknown men's clothing? Nowadays nobody gave anything away to anyone! And what should she answer if she were asked *who* they were for?

A hopeless venture. As she realised this, the fear rose up again, hitting her in the stomach. Before she left, she stuck the calendar in her coat pocket too.

A sharp wind was blowing as she set off. Down at the bridge she heard someone calling her name from a distance. Felix, in his uniform! He was running out of the village. She held her breath.

'Where are you going?' he asked in astonishment when he caught up with her.

'To walk for a bit,' she answered as casually as possible. 'I'll be back by lunchtime.'

'Wait a minute,' he said, 'I'll just get changed and come with you.'

'Let me go on my own,' she begged. 'I need peace, I want to write a poem, you see.'

That had always been her argument when she wanted to get rid of him.

'You and your poems,' he said annoyed and turned round. 'They're more important to you than I am...'

When she had got over the bridge and was trudging into the wood, he called after her: 'And what's in the rucksack?'

'A change of shoes', she answered. 'In case I get my feet wet. And something to eat. Satisfied?'

'Why don't you take a whole furniture lorry while you're at it!' he shouted spitefully.

She saw that he was standing in front of the house and staring after her. So she set off in a different direction and went a long way round.

She'd have to be on her guard against Felix. So far he didn't seem to have any suspicions. But he'd become curious.

And there was always the fear, the horrible fear!

By the time Anna reached the bunker there was driving snow. The storm was blowing the flakes deep into the passage. Knocking out her signal, she walked into the darkness, and found the entrance to the Russian's hiding place without difficulty. He was waiting for her. He had put the pillow on a flat block of rubble and now he gestured to her to sit on it. She did so, but reluctantly. On his pillow! She pulled the calendar out of her pocket, unfolded it and showed it to him. He held it right up to his eyes and quickly grasped what it was. When she pointed to the third Sunday in December he nodded. Gratefully he took the calendar and leant it up in a niche in the wall.

How on earth could the man manage in this cold without becoming ill? She was freezing in here. He'd probably got used to the cold in the prison camp. And to such winter temperatures. When Seff was last on leave he'd told her that it was unbelievable what people can get used to.

To temperatures far below minus twenty degrees, for example. Or to wearing the same clothes for days on end until everything stuck to you and stank. And to being so hungry that you'd feed yourself on dog or even rat meat. History showed that. In besieged fortresses, for example. Things like that were said to happen in Russian prison camps too.

'Could you eat dogs and rats?' she had asked him in horror.

'Of course,' he had answered calmly. 'If it was a matter of survival. You could too.'

'Never!' she had shouted, repulsed.

He had only laughed at that – and then admitted that

even he had got used to unbelievable things in Russia. Such as emptying his mess tin next to fallen soldiers.

After that conversation, she hadn't been able to eat a mouthful at supper. And for days she had seen her brother with different eyes. Had he lost all feeling? How could you spoon up your food next to dead bodies, maybe of people you'd known?

Perhaps in war, very slowly, very gradually, you got accustomed to inhumanity, became deadened? Perhaps even Germans got accustomed to wreaking dreadful havoc, out there in enemy lands. Perhaps even Seff?

No. Not him. Eating next to corpses, that must be the worst he was capable of ...

The worst? He killed people! After all, that was what he was there for. Well, they were enemies. But still people!

Hurriedly she emptied her rucksack and laid it all out on the floor: rolls, dripping and candles, apples, cake and dried pears, prunes, the *Blutwurst*.

Then something happened which she was totally unprepared for. The Russian bent down, snatched up the sausage, grasped it with both hands and bit into it without peeling it first. He just bit through the skin. The sausage meat sprayed out, on the wall, on Seff's jacket, Seff's trousers. She saw the man chew, swallow, smack his lips. Dark red lumps hung from his chin, his lips.

The Russian on the poster had looked like that: blood on his hands, his clothes, his lips. Unbounded greed. The only thing missing was the knife in his mouth!

He looked up and met Anna's horrified gaze. Then he put the rest of the sausage back down on the floor and wiped his mouth. Disgustedly she pointed to the jacket and trousers. She saw his embarrassment. He reached for the kitchen knife and scraped the sticky mess off his chest and leg. Spots remained though. He scratched longer than necessary. He was obviously trying not to have to look at Anna. But now he had a knife in his hand too! Hastily she stood up, drew back, the pillow fell on the floor.

But that was all nonsense. She was imagining things. He wouldn't saw off the branch he was sitting on. In his present situation, he was totally dependent on her. She looked around. Among all the things that could betray her, wasn't there something or other that she could take home? She pointed to one of the sacks. He nodded anxiously, put the knife back in the alcove, fetched the potato sack from the next room as well, shook both the sacks out, folded them together and handed them to her. Then he reached for the torch and went ahead of her out into the darkness.

She felt oppressed again. Just get out of the bunker, just get away! But he didn't turn round once, just strode swiftly on, without having to support himself, without swaying. As if merely being full had given him strength. The *Blutwurst*. His whole stomach was full of *Blutwurst*. She felt ill, just from thinking about it.

On arriving in the main corridor, he wanted to go with her to the exit but she waved him away vigorously. He stood there with hanging arms. '*Spassibo*,' he said quietly. After a few steps she turned round again and shone the torch on him. He was still standing there. She turned around and went.

She longed for daylight and fresh air. Out, just get out of

there! Her steps echoed through the passage. As it got light around her, she was hit by a squall of snow. Outside the storm was raging. Only in the open, in the middle of the snowstorm, did she stuff the sacks back in the rucksack. She wanted to smuggle one straight back into the cellar. She'd have to hide the other one though, until she'd got all the things from the attic together.

As she walked down the slope through the storm, a great depression came over her. Quite apart from the clothes she had to get hold of – how could she keep getting food? Anything filling was rationed.

Certainly nobody at home was suffering from hunger, because there were still the hens, goats and rabbits and the big garden and orchards. And there was the Lamb with its leftovers. But to supply an extra adult man, and above all secretly, that was practically impossible. And how could she go up there at least once a week without being noticed?

But she couldn't just let him starve. And he wasn't yet strong enough to get further away. For that she would have to carry on feeding him up a bit longer. A vicious circle!

As she left the forest, she came up against the storm which crashed into her. She had to bend right down to be able to move forwards. There were snowdrifts right across the bridge. Thick flakes whirled in her face.

Suddenly she jumped. Someone was standing in front of her. Felix.

'I was just coming to look for you,' he shouted reproachfully. And then he added gloatingly: 'Serves you right!'

9

It was to be a short but wildly eventful week for Anna. It even began quite disturbingly on Sunday evening on the journey to Schonberg. She was sitting with two service-men and an old woman in a dimly lit compartment. One of the servicemen, a sailor, really wanted to talk to her. He seemed to be at least twice her age. He asked her quite openly if she had a boyfriend already. And if she knew how to kiss. She found the way he looked at her impudent.

The other man got out. Two stops later, the old woman left the compartment too. The sailor grinned at Anna, sat down next to her, put his arm around her and said: 'So, now let's make ourselves comfortable, shall we?'

And he already had his hand under her skirt.

She gave him a resounding slap, jumped up, grabbed her bags and stormed into a compartment where two women were sitting with a couple of children. There she drew out a schoolbook and started reading, to take her mind off it. But the letters swam before her eyes. Apart from that, the lamp was dimmed, like all the lamps in the train. So it was too dark to read.

How greedily he had made up to her. Disgusting. In contrast, the greed of the Russian yesterday had been harmless. Just hunger, wild hunger! In the same situation Seff would probably have pounced on the sausage like that. And if she, as a Russian woman in a

Russian train, had been bothered like that by a German soldier? Would she have been allowed to defend herself? And if so – what would the consequences have been?

She had a key to the Beraneks' front door. Frau Beranek looked out of the sitting room as Anna came into the hall. 'It's good to see you,' she said quietly. 'I still can't sleep. And on my own like that, the thoughts come. I've still got a bit of cake. I was given it this afternoon. Would you like some? Come in...'

Frau Beranek snuggled into one corner of the sofa with her knees drawn up; Anna pressed herself into the other because mending was piled up on the armchair. Probably Frau Beranek made these sad days bearable by throwing herself into her work, like so many women who had been informed that their husbands and sons were dead. Anna looked her over surreptitiously. She had become thin, and the black clothes made her seem older than she was. Gisela Beranek, widow.

'You can relax a bit,' she said and passed Anna the plate with the cake. 'You're quite tense.'

Anna took a slice and ate. Coffee-grounds-cake with artificial marzipan. On another day she would have been glad of a second helping. But today, after all that – and here with the grieving woman...

She remembered that Grandmother had slipped in a *Blutwurst* when saying goodbye. 'For Frau Beranek, the poor woman. Offer her our deepest sympathy...'

Frau Beranek was pleased with the present and carried it into the kitchen. 'Your grandmother must have a good heart,' she said as she came back.

Yes, that was true. In spite of the business with the plants out of the Grünbaums' garden.

A heavy silence fell. Anna stared absent-mindedly at the bookcase.

'Would you like to borrow something to read?' asked Frau Beranek.

'Have you got anything about Russ...?' asked Anna and broke off, shocked, in the middle of the word. Had she given too much away?

'About Russians?' Frau Beranek asked quietly in return. 'But of course. Tolstoy, for example. Gogol. Gorky. Dostoevsky. Any amount. My husband is...' She corrected herself: 'My husband was a bookworm, and I sometimes devour a book in one night too.'

She went to the bookcase, came back with a volume and gave it to Anna. She read: *Crime and Punishment*.

It was all the same to Anna who had written it. The names that Frau Beranek had just mentioned were all strange to her.

'As I told you before,' Frau Beranek said, 'the Russians are no worse than we are.'

Anna felt like a – she couldn't have described it. The closest would be: like a balloon, blown up almost to bursting point. If she could only speak about what was worrying her! Then she would be relieved of the pressure, the tension, the unbearable burden!

She threw her hands up over her face and burst into tears. Frau Beranek slid over to her and took her in her arms.

'First have a good cry,' she whispered in her ear, 'and

then tell me about it, if you want to.'

Anna kept silent.

'Have you had some bad news too?'

Anna shook her head.

'Even without getting news of somebody's death anyone could burst out crying at any time,' said Frau Beranek. 'Over the crazy war. And because of all the injustice that happens in our country without us making a sound. Over the guilt that we are loading ourselves up with, because we don't yell Stop! And put a stop to the *Gröfaz*!'

Gröfaz. That expression was known in Stiegnitz too, but it was only whispered behind people's hands: Greatest *Führer* of all time. Anna knew who was meant by that word. And *how* it was meant. But what did Frau Beranek mean by the injustice that she spoke of? Did she mean that you weren't allowed to say what you thought? And that they had been cruel to the Jews? And what was she accusing Hitler of? That he had taken on too much with this war? That had happened to many commanders and kings and *Kaisers* in the past. That was like chess. But the war wasn't over yet. Perhaps Hitler would get lucky again, now with the Ardennes offensive for example!

Oh, Anna was sick and tired of all the politics, she never wanted to hear about it again. For her there was now only *one* problem, which took up all her time, and she didn't know... she didn't know...

'I need men's clothes, warm ones,' it burst out of her. 'And blankets. And a cup and a saucepan and...'

'Ssh!' said Frau Beranek. And then, so casually, as if it was just a matter of course: 'Is there only one, or are there several?'

'One,' sobbed Anna.

'Just one. Well, if it's nothing more. The man can be helped. Is he big, small, fat, thin?'

Frau Beranek asked for a list of the necessary things. And she added: 'My husband would definitely have agreed to me giving away things from his wardrobe for something like this.'

She didn't ask any other questions.

Anna felt wonderfully relieved. She hadn't betrayed the place where the Russian was staying, his hiding place, and despite that, she had still got clothes for him. It couldn't have gone any better. She was eternally grateful to Frau Beranek!

She wrote out the list late that night in her attic. It was so cold in the room that she was breathing out white steam. Her fingers were quite stiff. But her elation warmed her. Now she would be able to exchange all the things that the Russian had in the bunker that could give her away.

She crawled into bed and began to read the book. It was so totally, totally different from Dwinger's books. This student Raskolnikov – what a man! A student in St Petersburg who lived in dreadful poverty, but still tried to help people who were even worse off. A Russian. A man who could unexpectedly get into a wild rage, but who showed a great deal of sensitivity at other times. A man who was basically good, but still capable of evil, full of contradictions.

She read until her eyes fell shut. That night she had nightmares.

On Monday morning, the death of Frau Murr, the sports teacher, was announced. The week before, she had taken two days' holiday to visit her husband who was seriously injured in a hospital in Cologne. On the way her train was bombed in a station. Her three-year-old son was also dead. Frau Murr had been very popular, and everyone had known her son too. An air of depression prevailed throughout the school, and when, as so often, there was an air-raid warning – normally no reason to panic, since they had always flown over Schonberg before – it gave rise to fear. As usual everyone went down into the cellar, but a few girls from the younger classes began to cry, one even had a screaming fit. Everyone, even the teachers, breathed out when the all clear came.

In the early afternoon, Anna took another look over the previous evening's list and gave it to Frau Beranek. Then she escaped under the warm blanket again and carried on reading. What an amazing world was opened to her there! That was the way Russians thought, acted, felt. The events narrated by this Dostoevsky were, admittedly, quite a while ago. Now new generations lived in Russia. In the Soviet Union. But they were Russians, surely their character had remained the same. She was so deep in the novel that she missed her piano lesson. She only finished her homework sketchily. When she came in from school on Tuesday, she found all kinds of things laid out on her bed: coat and trousers, a pullover and scarf, men's

91

underwear, socks, rubber boots, a cap. As well as that, a sleeping bag. Also a saucepan, cutlery and a cup. And even two plates, that hadn't been on the list at all.

Anna was so happy that she had to run downstairs on the spot, and flung her arms around Frau Beranek's neck.

'It's not new, any of that,' said Frau Beranek, 'but it's still good. It's only shoes that I can't get. They're bound to be too small for the man. You see, for his size, my husband had peculiarly small...'

She threw herself onto the sofa and began to cry. Anna sat down next to her and shyly touched her hand – in the same way that the Russian in the hayloft had touched *her* hand. Frau Beranek blew her nose and sat up again. 'Sometimes it just gets too much for me,' she sobbed. 'But the boots are two sizes bigger. Because he had thick woollen socks in them in winter, for shovelling snow...'

With a shake, she lifted her head and looked at Anna: 'Do you know just what you're doing there?'

Anna felt the blood draining from her face. She nodded.

'And if the situation is what I think it is,' Frau Beranek continued, 'do you also know what you could be in for, if it all comes out?'

Anna stared at her and nodded. 'I didn't know at first. I was just sorry for him, and so I helped him. I've found out since then. But I can't just let him starve now.'

'No, you can't do that,' said Frau Beranek seriously. 'I couldn't do that either. *If* you were capable of leaving him in trouble, you wouldn't have been sorry for him. Have you hidden him well?'

Anna nodded.

'And you're terribly careful when you go to him, and when you come from him?'

Anna nodded.

'And your family aren't at all suspicious?'

'Not so far. But...'

'Would they give you away? I mean, is there someone among them who wouldn't keep quiet?'

'They'd all keep quiet,' said Anna. 'Apart from my younger brother. He would be capable of...'

'He believes all that stuff about allegiance and the duty towards the Fatherland, doesn't he? Poor boy.'

There was a long pause. Then Frau Beranek said: 'Risky, the whole thing. And if you're found out, then I'm in trouble too.'

'I'll never betray you!' cried Anna.

'I believe you,' said Frau Beranek. 'But if it comes to that, then you won't be in control any longer. Well, never mind. If I got caught, then I'd just have been unlucky. But you, child...' She put her arm around Anna. 'Fear, isn't it? I can see it in your face. I've come to know it too. Fear for my husband. If you push it down by day, then it spreads out at night. It poisons everything.'

Anna laid her head on Frau Beranek's shoulder and let the tears flow silently.

The rucksack wasn't big enough for all the luggage. The suitcase that Anna always travelled to Schonberg with at the beginning of term was also filled up. Now, at the beginning of the Christmas holidays, she wouldn't stand out with so much luggage. But would she be able to carry it all? After all there would be her schoolbag and shopping bag as well!

She would *have* to be able to carry it! For as long as Seff's and Grandmother's and Grandfather's things were still in the bunker, it was as if she was living on hot coals!

She saw that all the name tags, all the labels had disappeared from Herr Beranek's things. Torn out, cut out. Neither did the name Schonberg appear anywhere. This stuff would betray nothing. Oh dear, good, wonderful Frau Beranek!

Even at the Wednesday evening meeting, in Anna's thoughts she was with Raskolnikov, the hero of her novel. His story almost overstretched her imagination – and fascinated her. In delirium, Raskolnikov had killed a disgusting old woman! A ghastly female, who, as a pawnbroker, became rich on the misery of others. So he was a murderer – but still no monster; yes, he was anything but a brute, he was a person with whom she, Anna, was living and suffering!

Compare that to this dreary singing. Anna liked to sing, and until now, she had been glad when singing, not political instruction, was the order of the day. But Raskolnikov, and all that was connected to him, were more important to her now.

There was a ceremony coming up and the *Führerin* was going to a lot of trouble to practise a difficult round for it with the group. Only a short time ago, Anna would have found it fun to get a grasp of this round. Now she was indifferent to it. Its text corresponded to the usual pattern: *Many must fall and pass into the grave, ere our destiny reached, the proud banners wave*...Of course there had to be banners. And it finished: *We hammer it home that all wealth and good, To be gained for the future must be earned through our blood*. Three groups had to sing through the melody half a bar of four-four time apart. The whole thing really did sound like hammering. Some people sang it wrongly, one group came off the rails all the time, and the *Führerin* was ashamed that she wasn't succeeding in drumming the song into her girls.

Anna looked over the text of the round again. It attempted to justify the host of soldiers' deaths with reaching their destiny. What did that really mean? Was there anything at all in the world that could justify so much violent death? And in the last lines she stumbled over the vocabulary: earned through blood. She'd never come across that idea before. *That all wealth and good, To be gained for the future must be earned through our blood*: a claim which could do with some evidence. Why shouldn't it be possible – for individuals as well as for a whole nation – to be happy without bloodshed?

'Now pull yourselves together!' snapped the *Führerin*.

Hardly was the meeting over, when Anna was in her room, reading more of the novel about Raskolnikov. In the middle of reading a thought struck her. Was this, Raskolnikov's Russia, the Russia that her Father had loved? He had been there during the Twenties. Since the time which was the background for the novel, certainly a lot had changed, and by no means always to the people's disadvantage. She had spoken about it with Frau Beranek. The other woman had been of the opinion that poverty as portrayed in the novel did not exist there any more. In the Soviet Union there were no starving students, and such greedy pawnbrokers as the one Raskolnikov killed would certainly have been stopped since then. But Russians who bared their souls, like Raskolnikov, who opened themselves up completely, were innocent and vulnerable, loved without holding anything back and could get into a reckless fury – there were surely still such Russians as those.

Was the man in the bunker like that too?

She slept badly. Lately she had often started awake with a scream. Afterwards she tossed and turned for hours, brooding.

Good and evil, grown tangled up together in every human being.

But what made people behave well or badly?

Would she too be capable of committing murder under certain circumstances?

On the next morning Anna went to school without any homework. Before the beginning of lessons she quickly copied down a couple of maths questions.

'What's wrong with you lately?' asked Sonja, who sat next to her, in amazement. 'Are you in love?'

Not in love, but deeply stirred up. More knowing and mature than even three weeks ago. And above all, more serious. After all, it wasn't a matter of good and evil. It was a matter of life and death.

*

And what should she give her landlady for Christmas now? After Herr Beranek's death, she could hardly turn up with the jack-in-the-box! And that would be too stingy as a present after this wonderful help. On the last evening before her journey home, Anna went downstairs to Frau Beranek and told her rather anxiously that she didn't have a present for her. At that Frau Beranek laughed and said that she knew a present that she would be glad of: for Anna to call her by her first name.

That was also a present for Anna.

On the Thursday morning, the last school day before the Christmas holidays she quickly darted in to see Gisela Beranek once more before school to say goodbye to her.

'Don't worry about a thing,' she whispered to her. 'If it gets found out, I'll never, never mention your name!'

'It's all right,' answered Gisela Beranek quietly, as she slipped into a dressing gown. 'Let's just trust to luck.'

They had got used to lowering their voices when discussing this topic.

'If a policeman looks in your suitcase on the way and is surprised,' said Gisela, 'then you must say that a war widow gave you her husband's things for bomb victims and refugees.'

She went with Anna as far as the garden gate. Anna was taking the luggage to school with her so as to be able to leave straight after lessons.

'By the way, Russians don't celebrate Christmas on the twenty-fourth of December, but on the seventh of January,' Gisela whispered to Anna. 'Just in case it happens to interest you.'

It interested her a great deal. 'Happy Christmas,' she croaked, struggling down the steps with her rucksack, schoolbag, shopping bag and suitcase.

Happy Christmas? For God's sake, what had she said there? After all, Herr Beranek was...

'It doesn't matter,' said Gisela. 'I nearly wished you one. At least we can still say that to children in these times. All the best. Take care of yourself.'

She stayed standing by the front door and watched after Anna, who turned round once more on the street and called back over the garden fence a muted, 'And thank you for everything!' She had never carried such heavy luggage before. She thought of a saying that hung in the room where League meetings took place: *Whatever doesn't kill me makes me stronger*... Who was it by? As things stood, probably by Hitler. After all sayings of his were hanging everywhere, his sayings were recited everywhere. But whoever it was by, she had to get the luggage home, no matter what it cost her. And so she clenched her teeth and dragged it further.

'Good God!' exclaimed Sonja, whom she met on the way. 'Are you moving house?' And she carried the schoolbag and shopping bag for her.

At school she wasn't the only heavily laden one. Many people were travelling home today. Today you stumbled over rucksacks, suitcases and bags everywhere.

The Christmas reports were given out. Hers wasn't as good as usual this time. Never before, in all the time she'd been at the grammar school, had she sunk so low: five Twos and even a Three!

What did it matter? In wartime there were more important things than school grades. Mother would, as always, put her signature on it in passing and remark: 'See to it that you work your way back up again.' Felix, who always envied all her many Ones, would gloat. And Grandmother? She would include her in her evening prayers.

After the final lesson she quickly bought a small loaf of bread, half a kilo of sugar and a hundred grams of margarine on the Bahnhofstrasse, all still on her ration card. She had been saving coupons lately: twice she hadn't been to the canteen, and she'd only eaten small amounts in the evenings.

And she wanted three onions. You didn't need coupons for those. And had any batteries come in, by any chance? Torch batteries? No? Pity.

At the station kiosk she had better luck: the last two.

This time, once again, she would arrive one train earlier in Mellersdorf, and again walk straight from the station up to the bunker. It was hazy. Perhaps it would snow.

Dear God, let it snow.

10

As Anna panted over the bridge at the end of Mellersdorf, a girl called out to her from a farm. Anna only knew her by sight. Fortunately she didn't ask anything but disappeared into the stable. After that she didn't meet anyone else until she reached the bunker entrance.

She was struggling. The luggage was so heavy. More and more often, she had to put down the suitcases and bags and rest for a while. She was leaving really very odd tracks. She hoped that no one would notice them. And it didn't seem to want to snow. So the tracks would be visible for a long time.

By now it had already become routine, this route through the long corridor, giving the agreed knocking signal. The Russian was waiting for her at the entrance to his rooms, made an inviting gesture and said something which sounded like 'Dobro pozhalovat'. If she'd been him, she would have said 'welcome' on such an occasion. Perhaps that was what it meant?

This time he seemed to be even happier that she had come than the last time. Had he been afraid that she wouldn't come any more? The pillow was already lying on the rubble for her.

As she unpacked he was astonished – and quickly understood that he should get changed. He withdrew into one of the other rooms and after a while appeared grinning in Herr Beranek's things. In comparison with before he looked really smart.

Anna pointed to the boots on his feet. She realised that he would have liked to keep them. But they were what mattered particularly to her.

Shrugging, he took them off. Gisela had added two pairs of thick hand-knitted socks. They were very warm too. And the rubber boots seemed to fit. Together they shook out the horse blanket, folded it up. The Russian wanted to roll up the rag rug too. But she waved him away. There were similar old, fraying rugs in every house in Stiegnitz and the neighbouring villages.

He was quite plainly amused by the sofa cushion. He placed it on the sleeping bag as if it were a sofa. And it *was* funny really: a sofa cushion in a place like this! But Gisela Beranek had given it as a pillow.

How cheerful he was today.

When Anna had packed everything up, including the pan and flowered cup, pillow and cutlery, she took the calendar out of the niche and looked at it. In two days' time, it was Christmas Eve. So she couldn't possibly leave the house without attracting attention. And not on Christmas Day or Boxing Day either. The first chance would be on one of the next weekdays. She pointed to the 27th and 28th December, gestured from one date to the other and shrugged.

He bent right down over the calendar. Couldn't he see very well? He seemed to understand what she meant because he nodded. At the same time, his arm touched hers. Hastily she stepped to the side. He glanced over to her, then looked away.

When Anna wanted to go he asked her with a hand gesture to wait a moment longer. He disappeared and came back with a wooden star, a star woven from splinters of wood. He pointed to the knife in the niche and to himself. Then he passed her the star. With his eyes pinched together, he looked at her expectantly. A present for her? A star! She tried to remember the word that she had heard so often from him now.

'*Spassibo*,' she said and looked at the star so as not to have to look him in the eye.

He went into another room and appeared with a piece of board about a hand span in length and width, a finger thick. He could only have found that somewhere in the bunker. Then he reached for the knife from the niche and carved splints from the narrow side, sending them flying. It was quite similar to the way Grandmother split kindling for the fire.

Engrossed, Anna watched him. He collected a handful of splinters and counted some of them out in Russian. There were eight. Then he laid two of them in a cross and another two in the gaps on top of them, crosswise once again. A middle point with eight rays. And now he wove another four splints between the beams – over, under, over – until the whole thing made a solid star, entwined together so that it didn't fall apart. Anna was amazed. He laughed quietly, pulled one piece, just one, out of the model and at once the star fell apart again.

He indicated the splints with his hand. Hesitantly she laid two on top of each other, then another two crosswise on top, in the holes. But now what? He pointed, she learned, and after a couple of failed efforts she'd figured it out. Admittedly her star was a bit wonky, but it was just a small matter to get it into shape.

What a present! Not just the star, but also how to make it. A little piece of magic. These would surely have entertained her father too.

But now she had to go. She stuck both their stars into the suitcase. He showed her his torch. Didn't she want to swap them? But she waved him away. It was an everyday lamp; there was one in practically every household.

'*Spassibo – danke,*' she said.

'*Danke,*' he repeated. '*Danke.*'

Suddenly he clutched at his chest, seemed to start, pointed to Anna's luggage, pulled out Seff's jacket and felt in the inside pocket. A postcard sized photograph, already somewhat worn, came to light. He showed it to her. She could recognise a family: a woman, a man, two sons, a daughter, all in loose summer things – the boys in short trousers – round a table in a garden. The woman – with glasses and waved hair – was maybe forty-five, perhaps only forty. Her flowery blouse was no different from the blouses worn by Mother, Hedi or Giscla Beranek. The woman didn't seem to be a worn out farmer's wife. She was laughing. The father too, also wearing glasses, was grinning into the lens. The person taking the photograph had probably cracked a joke. She knew people did that.

How old would the three young people be? Twenty,

eighteen, twelve? Give or take a year or two. In any case the girl looked a lot younger than her brothers. She had blonde pigtails. The whole family seemed to be blond. The father was tall and stately, the mother almost gaunt.

The Russian pointed to the younger son and then to himself.

'Maxim,' he said. Then he gave a second and third name. His surname? But the third – did people in Russia have *three* names? She thought about Dostoevsky's Raskolnikov. Yes: the Christian name, the father's name, the surname.

So he was called Maxim. She handed him back the photo. Now he must be expecting her to introduce herself too. She hesitated. Should she give her real name? If he was caught and interrogated, they might make him betray it.

'Eva,' she said and pointed to herself. How quickly that name had come to mind! Eva – after all, that was what her father had wanted to name her.

The Russian looked up in surprise. 'Adam? – Yeva?' he asked.

She nodded. Then he pulled the photo out again and pointed to his sister. 'Yeva,' he said beaming. When he laughed the ugly gap in his teeth became visible. The upper left canine tooth was missing. And so was the corner of the incisor next to it. She noticed a deep scar on his upper lip among the sprouting hairs.

Yeva. That must be Eva. So his sister had the same name as her. Or rather, the name she should have had.

He helped her with her luggage nearly all the way to

the bunker entrance. When he was walking next to her like that and lighting her feet she felt no fear at all. Neither of him, nor of discovery.

Now she had exchanged the things, suspicion would no longer fall on her – if nobody caught her on the way to him. But now it was possible for him to go! Perhaps another week or two until he was back to strength to some extent. But until then, she wouldn't abandon him. The Russian was no longer just somebody. From now on he was Maxim.

It was snowing as she left the bunker. Good. Her tracks, and above all those from the luggage, would soon be invisible.

The luggage was hardly any lighter than before, but at least she was going downhill. She would get home at the usual time.

Grandmother, at home alone, had a lot to tell her. Hans-Joachim Hanisch, a grandson of her sister who lived in the next village, had been killed. And the youngest of the Graulichs, only just eighteen, and Werner Schmied from Mellersdorf, the father of four children. He was supposed to have said to his wife on his last leave: 'I won't come home again.'

'And just imagine, Hedi is pregnant! When it's three years since her husband fell. And she won't tell anyone, not even your mother, who the father is. And nobody's seen her with anyone. Your mother will soon have to keep an eye out for some help!'

That's how they were, the old wives of Stiegnitz: if there was a secret, they sniffed around tirelessly until they'd found it out. Only very few pairs of lovers managed to escape their attention. Poor Hedi. Now tongues in Stiegnitz were wagging over her.

And yet these days there was so much that was much more important to talk about, if you felt like speaking at all. Every day new reports came from the Ardennes front, reports of advances, of successes. And you could talk about the Eastern Front too, about the straightening and shortening of the front. Even Grandmother understood perfectly well what that meant. But she only spoke about the Front in connection with Seff.

Anna waited until Grandmother was in the stable. Then she threw the cutlery into the drawer of the kitchen cupboard, got the potato sack and pan into the cellar, carried the pillow into the attic and Seff's things into the boys' room. She was careful to make sure that everything went back into the right place in Seff's wardrobe, although it was dirty and smelled of smoke. After the war was over, Seff would be bound to wonder about the unwashed things in his cupboard, but there would no longer be any danger for her, Anna. When Grandmother came back into the living room, Anna had piled the boots, sack and blanket on the table.

'All there!' she cried triumphantly. 'The cleaner had stuck the things in the broom cupboard. Nobody thought of looking in there!'

'Well, there you are then!' Grandmother clapped her hands together. 'See how things sort themselves out with God's help.'

The flowered cup was there too. Frau Beranek had

given it back to her. In return for the *Blutwurst*. And she said thank you very much.

Grandmother was deeply moved. A while later when she wanted to chop onions for supper she was amazed by the return of the kitchen knife. She'd been looking for that for a long time.

Very high spirits. But then when Felix came home, Anna faced another dangerous moment. Because after he'd gone up to the boys' room, he came crashing down again at once and shouted: 'Someone's been in my room! I shut the door earlier. Now it's half open. And it smells different in there!'

Anna decided to take the bull by the horns.

'I was in your room,' she said quietly. 'Because I thought you were there. I was disgustingly sweaty from walking.'

'Did you look under my bed?' he asked threateningly.

So that was what was bothering him. She began to laugh with relief. He must have hidden something there. Probably a present.

'I'm afraid not,' she retorted. 'But I will now!'

There was a wild tussle and screaming until the crockery in the kitchen cupboard began to rattle, Felix's uniform shirt came untucked from his trousers and Grandmother separated them with the dishcloth.

She kept shouting: 'Don't be so childish, you two!'

11

Three days later, on Christmas Eve, Anna got to see what Felix had been hiding under his bed: an extremely pretty sewing box with two folding trays.

'All done with the fretsaw,' he reported proudly. 'I've been slaving away over that since October!'

Across the two lids, burned darkly into the wood, it said: *To Anna, From Felix*. God knows that was a present that he could boast about a bit. She on the other hand was ashamed. All she had for him was this measly packet of target sheets. What else could she do but hug him and declare that he was the best brother in the world?

He beamed. That wasn't the only reason that he was the happiest member of the family this evening: he had received not only the air rifle he had been longing for, but also one of Uncle Franz's puppies. And for the rest of the Christmas holiday – there was no Hitler Youth service – he did nothing but alternate between shooting the targets on the barn wall with the air rifle and playing with the puppy, which he named Donar. Donar, the Germanic god of thunder: a name which inspired respect.

Anna had received lovely presents from Mother, Grandmother and Uncle Franz too: a photo album; perfume; sewing thread and bed linen, damask, still brand new but twenty years old, from Grandmother's supply. 'For your bottom drawer.' Grandmother had saved all her life for when times were hard.

'I wonder what next Christmas Eve will be like for us?' Mother asked, dropping the question into the middle of the candlelight and the aroma from the cakes.

'Be quiet!' cried Grandmother, really angry. 'You're ruining the lovely Christmas mood for us!'

Since her return, Maxim's star had been hanging from a thread on the lamp in Anna's room. And now, late on Christmas Eve, Anna sat on the floor with Felix, and demonstrated how to make that sort of star in an instant. She cut splints from a board and wove them together. There, another star!

Felix was amazed and let her show him how to do it.

'Who showed you that?' he asked.

'A school friend,' answered Anna lightly.

Even Mother managed to make one, and thought they would be a pretty, cheap Christmas decoration for the Lamb. They would look impressive in a long row on the wall for example.

'We used to make stars like that when I was a child,' remembered Grandmother. 'There was a fashion for them then. I think it came from Russia. Because we called the things Russian Stars...'

Anna felt the blood rush to her head. She kept her head bowed, seeming engrossed in making the stars and didn't dare to breathe.

'Oh well,' said Felix, pushing his star to one side and standing up, 'the thing's rather primitive actually. Nothing but splints.'

When she went to her room later that evening, she threw herself onto her bed, linked her arms behind her head and looked up at her father.

You knew it too, she thought, this problem of good and bad. If you were still alive, you could see it in your son. In Felix, whom you never knew. He's convinced that anything that benefits the German people is good. But he lets others dictate what that is. No, he's not someone who only thinks of his own advantage. If it were demanded of him to die for Germany, he would do it as a matter of course. But he leaves it to others to decide for him what's good and what's bad. That's why I'm afraid of him, Father. I'm afraid of my little brother!

Perhaps you thought you weren't needed here, my Marie is so capable, she'll manage on her own. But you were needed very much, Father. For Felix above all. Because he's made of the same stuff as you. While he was still young, you would have shown him that there are things in the world, other than the Fatherland and the petty-minded people of Stiegnitz, which are worth living for. And that you shouldn't just let yourself be carried along by the herd – be drawn along without using your brain or your heart. No matter whether the herd is just made up of non-political villagers, or whether the swastika is carried before them.

Ever since he was little, no one has had time for Felix – apart from those who have made him what he is: a blind, fanatical Hitler Youth.

You would have had time for him. And I would have needed you very much just now. I could have told *you*, the Abracadabra, the lunatic, about the Russian in the bunker. Together with you, Father, everything would have been much easier for me...

She decided to give Maxim something too – for *his* Christmas! A present that would bring him joy.

Her first thought was cigarettes. He would certainly be glad of them. But the smell might give him away. And anyway, Grandmother always sent the family's entire cigarette ration to Seff. No, the present for Maxim must not cause any kind of disadvantage to Seff.

Then she thought of the harmonica that Seff had once given her. She had never played it. But Seff's present – she couldn't give that away to Maxim! In any case, sounds could also give him away.

Boots? They would be incredibly valuable in the cold of the bunker. But they were only available on coupons, if at all.

In the end, an idea came to her, which took her breath away. From his point of view it must be *the* present. It didn't smell, made no noise and she could get it without coupons. It would help him to pass the time and definitely give him hope, above all hope.

But from her point of view: no. That bordered on – on what? She couldn't go that far!

She had secretly fished Felix's map out of the chest drawer, together with the little flags, and held it up to the light in her room. The holes from the flag pins could still be seen clearly. What a huge area they enclosed. From the North Cape to Africa, from Normandy to the Urals.

And now? During the last few months, she hadn't

wanted to know at all where the fronts ran. But in the next few days she listened very carefully to all the military reports and noted all the places which were named. In her room she bent over the map and sought them out.

There was hardly any talk of the Ardennes offensive any longer. As long ago as last October, the Russians had temporarily penetrated into East Prussia, had had to withdraw and now were finally stationed on the East Prussian border. And day by day, the enemy armies were getting closer, in Italy and the Balkans too. For the first time, Anna became shockingly aware of how encircled Germany had now become. She had avoided taking in these developments for such a long time. Now the recognition of the Germans' hopeless military position hit her like a thunderbolt. Only a fraction of the former conquests were still in German hands. And soon perhaps only half of Germany itself. Americans in Mainz, Russians in Berlin – unimaginable!

And to make this looming defeat known to the Russian?

No! Then there would be no turning back!

Right in the middle of the area still free of the enemy lay Stiegnitz, well protected, untouched. So far. A matter of time. What would become of her and her family when the war reached this far? Would they become refugees too then, like the women and children from the *Ruhrgebiet* who were stationed here? And what – if she had one at all – would her future be like?

In the last few days of 1944, Anna's faith in the

Führer and his Final Victory began to waver. In Felix, it burned brighter than ever.

He practised and practised with the air rifle. Just a couple of days after Christmas he demonstrated his skill, at a distance of five metres from the barn wall. He shot twelve times, all his shots hit the target, four even hit the three innermost rings. Grandmother clasped her hands together – as always in such circumstances. Even Mother was amazed. But she didn't have much time for that, she had to go to the Lamb to keep an eye on five French prisoners of war, who had been stationed there for today as workers. Bulky sheets of ice from the village ponds had to be got down to the cellars. That was always a laborious and time-consuming procedure.

'And you?' Felix turned to Anna, after Mother had gone and Grandmother was back in the house. 'Aren't you amazed?'

'I'm flabbergasted,' she said.

'As a sniper,' he grinned, 'I'll wipe them out in rows!'

'Who?' asked Anna.

'Stupid question. Russians of course! Bang, bang, bang.'

Anna was furious: 'You're treating people like animals!'

'I was talking about Russians,' answered Felix darkly. 'Wash your ears out!'

'You little monster,' said Anna with a cutting voice.

'Less of the "little",' answered Felix, equally cutting.

The war was still a long way off, even if not nearly as far as a year, or even a couple of weeks ago. But already, ever darker shadows were falling over Stiegnitz. All the older men were called up. From January they said that there would be even less fat available on the coupons. Lately Alois Straka, one of the few Czechs in the village, had been wearing a broad grin whenever he was seen in the Kirchplatz. And old Boena Lammer, a Czech despite her German name, now walked through the village with her head held high. She had been almost subservient to the German villagers since the annexation of the Sudetenland to Germany, but now she was extremely opinionated when she shopped in the dairy or the shops.

And the death notices seemed to double.

After Christmas, while Felix was helping in the Lamb, Anna walked back up to the bunker to take Maxim the batteries that she had forgotten last time as well as more provisions. At the last moment she added a hiking map.

He would be able to make it through to the Protectorate with that. He could find all the forest paths on it, all the streams, all the mountains and valleys, recognise the position of the southern villages.

This time Maxim wasn't waiting for her out in the corridor. When she had made her way to him, puzzled, she found him lying on the sleeping bag, the coat spread out over him, his arms behind his head. He hardly looked up as she entered his room. His hair was dishevelled, his eyes were red. As she bent over him, he turned his face to the wall.

While she was still unpacking the things she had

114

brought, he began to yell. They weren't words that he was shouting. He was just making noises, inarticulate screams.

He roared like an animal.

Suddenly he jumped up, grabbed the coat, the sleeping bag, hurled them against the wall, pulled the rag rug from the floor and threw it back down again so that clouds of dust flew up.

Horrified Anna pressed herself against the wall. She couldn't believe what she was seeing. Roaring, the man kicked the blocks of rubble, the rucksack, drummed his fists on the concrete wall, beat his head against the wall again and again, until he gradually quietened down.

She had fled to the next room, torn between fear and pity. She saw him fall to his knees, then let himself fall completely. Now he was lying stretched out full length on the floor, his arms spread out wide, just sobbing.

That noise must have been heard all the way outside – not through the main entrance, but through the blast holes.

If someone had heard it, what would he have thought it was? A wild animal? A madman?

If that caused someone to investigate, Maxim would be lost.

Run away from the bunker now? She couldn't. She couldn't leave him lying there like that.

She was fairly certain that it had been prison madness. Like prisoners sometimes got when isolated in solitary confinement. Seff had told of such an incident from his time in barracks. One of his comrades – she couldn't remember why – had been sentenced to a week in the guardhouse. After a couple of days he had suddenly begun to throw a fit.

Maxim was lying motionless now. Anna came out of the next room again, spread the rug out, laid the rolled up sleeping bag on it, the coat next to it. Then she looked for a cup and filled it with water. Ready to have to jump up at any time and get to safety, she knelt down next to him. The cup in her hand was shaking.

'Maxim,' she whispered.

He sat up. His hair was hanging madly in his face; his forehead, and his knuckles were bleeding. As he drank, he kept his eyes fixed on Anna. Then he put the cup down, hissed something that she didn't understand and made hefty movements towards the door opening, which could only mean 'Out!'

She grabbed the rucksack, tipped all the remaining contents out onto the ground, left the things she had already unpacked lying as they were, tore the torch out of her coat pocket and ran. As she hastened through the dark corridor, which today seemed to her to go on forever, she panted over and over: 'That's it.'

It wasn't until she had reached the bridge that she had herself under control to some extent. It was only her heart that was still pounding. She went straight to the Lamb. There was no Grandmother there who could tell at a glance when something was the matter with her. And Felix would certainly not have time to observe her too closely either, because he had to help out. There, by helping out herself, she would be able to digest what she had just experienced in the most unobtrusive way. As

116

she was hanging her empty rucksack and her coat on a hook in the hall, Felix came past, with a white apron on, three empty beer glasses in his hand. With a quick sideways glance at the coat and rucksack he said dryly: 'Do you need provisions then?'

This question caught her so much by surprise that she needed a while to think of an answer. Carefully suppressing her shock, she played for time: 'What do you mean? Provisions? I'm not going anywhere!'

'Why did you bring the rucksack then?'

By now she had herself in hand again: 'Because I thought there might be something to carry home this evening. Sometimes I even think ahead, unlike you.' She pulled the torch from her coat and shone it in his face. That was a reference to the previous evening when Felix had left his torch behind and, on the way home together, had had to rely on the light from hers.

He disappeared without a word. Her knees were trembling.

But let him be suspicious, let him sniff around after her – she'd had enough. Enough of the crazy fear, enough of the constant worry. Where can I get something to eat? And how do I get up to the bunker, and back down again, unseen? He had thrown her out, so she was free of all responsibility for him. He can look after himself alone! she thought furiously.

But as she washed the cutlery in the kitchen, she ran through the events in the bunker once again. There was no doubt that he had wanted her to go. Had he no longer been in his right mind? Suddenly she froze. Perhaps –

perhaps at that moment, totally beside himself, he hadn't been able to trust himself any longer? Perhaps he had chased her out so as to protect her from himself? After such a long time without a woman, had he simply not been able to – no. In that case, he'd already have shown that sort of desire. And she'd been expecting it. But he had always acted properly. He'd never given her any reason for worry, for fear.

Had it been a sudden explosion of rage, resulting in him hitting out senselessly at his surroundings? Rage at his almost hopeless situation, at his helplessness, at the person keeping him alive?

It wasn't her that he hated, but his unbearable dependence on her! Yes, she could empathise with that feeling. She could remember that as a child, after weeks of a serious illness, she had felt almost an enjoyment in tormenting Grandmother, who had tenderly nursed her day and night. Perhaps it made you aggressive to know you were so deeply indebted to someone else?

If that was what it was, then she mustn't leave him to himself! Then he was ill. Then, as Grandmother would say, he had soul trouble.

At the beginning of January several more bombed out families were billeted on the village, although Uncle Franz had already had trouble accommodating five dozen Berliners in the previous November.

Three families from Castrop-Rauxel were now lodging in guest rooms at the Lamb. Everyone had to help moving the furniture in the rooms and taking care of the distraught women, even Anna. Some of them had no more luggage than the clothes they were wearing.

While she was working at the Lamb, Anna wore her trousers with the deep pockets and a loose, baggy pullover, with one of Grandmother's overalls on the top. She made the most of every opportunity to let anything edible disappear into her pockets.

Soon she had reached the point of unconsciously checking almost everything that she did, for whether it could serve to provide food, and if so, how.

She was on her guard. Above all, she kept an eye on Felix. On suitable occasions, she complained to him that she had been so hungry lately. She always had an appetite. She had even nibbled at things in the dining room! Why should that be? Perhaps she was coming up to a growth spurt?

Now if he should come across bits of food in her pockets, it would no longer surprise him and lead him to wonder in dangerous directions. Or so she hoped.

These days, her thoughts kept coming back to Maxim. What had been going on in him, before he began to throw the fit? She tried to put herself in his position. Living like that up in the bunker must be really dreadful. She would probably have got into a rage like that even sooner.

And before? Maybe even his time as a soldier had seemed unbearable? How much more then must he have suffered from the life in the prison camp! He had looked half-starved when she had found him in the hay. Had he already been so famished, so dirty, even before his escape from the camp?

She wondered how old he was. And what he did. She tried to imagine him baking bread, waiting at tables, driving a tractor, sitting behind a post office counter. Did he like reading? Had he read *Crime and Punishment*? Oh, if only everybody spoke the same language! Then everything would be so much easier. Then she'd know what he was and how he had lived, until he had to become a soldier, how he felt and what he needed.

But there was one thing she knew even so. He needed hope.

So she decided with a heavy heart that she would take him the big map after all. With the little flags.

12

Every day, Grandmother watched for the postman and whenever she saw him coming up the slope, she ran towards him.

'Still nothing from Seff?'

'Still nothing.'

Grandmother could no longer think of anything else. Seff's letter was already over a week late. Holy Mother of God! Mother, on the other hand, very seldom spoke of Seff, almost as if she believed that just mentioning his name would bring him into danger.

On New Year's Eve, Mother shut the bar. There was no reason to celebrate the arrival of the new year. It was awaited with fear. And in any case, there would only have been a few alcoholics and loners hunched over their beers.

So it happened that Mother actually sat with Grandmother, Felix and Anna for a whole evening. But the mood was depressed. They were all thinking about Seff. Mother dug out the ludo set on the grounds that 'they should take their minds off it'. They played unenthusiastically. Grandmother was first to lose.

'It's because of the war that I've lost,' she complained. And then, even louder, as in an explosion: 'If only it was finally over – whatever happens!'

Yes. That was exactly it. Anna nodded to her. She had

never been aware of that wish before. But now Grandmother's outburst had planted it firmly in her mind. Defeat was already looming in any case. If they were going to lose the war, then let it happen as quickly as possible. So that Seff would finally be out of danger!

And Maxim.

And she herself.

But now Felix came to life. He jumped up and shouted at Grandmother: 'What do you mean "whatever happens"? You surely don't want the Russians to win! Do you?'

'I want Seff to stay alive!' she cried and burst into tears.

Felix looked at her scornfully: 'You still don't get it – life is not the most important thing.'

'What *is* most important then?' asked Mother.

'Well, the Fatherland of course! The Fatherland!' shouted Felix heatedly. 'And this war is a holy war! Against the Bolsheviks, against the subhuman races! It's lucky that not all Germans are as feeble as you lot. Otherwise the Final Victory would really be in danger!'

He turned to Anna: 'Let the old people falter – but you! Why you? You've learnt the same as me! That we must defeat the Reds! It's a matter of the future of Germany, the future of the whole of Europe! Everyone must stand together, must give their all, even their lives! But you – you think the Russians are people the same as us, and read Russian books and accept that the Russians will win the war and ... and ... '

He stared at her furiously. Now she was furious too. So he was poking around in her room. Yes, she had brought the Dostoevsky book home with her, with

Gisela's permission, to read it again, and she had carelessly put it on her bedside table.

'... and you're not prepared to risk your life either!'

'Stay out of my room!' she flung at him. 'I don't poke around in *your* things!'

'It's not about your room, it's about Germany!'

'That's enough,' said Mother and pulled Felix back into his chair.

'Well in any case, he can rely on me, the *Führer*,' said Felix, with a trembling voice. 'To death.'

He was dripping with sweat.

'You children can be really terrifying sometimes,' murmured Grandmother, blowing her nose.

On the morning of the seventh of January, Anna waited until Felix had gone to do his Duty, then ran off with the rucksack. The sun shimmered through the clouds. *If* Maxim was expecting her, then it would be today at the earliest. By the time she had already reached the bridge, someone called to her from behind. Felix came running after her. She began to feel queasy.

'Are you going walking again?' he grinned. 'I'll come with you. The meeting is cancelled this morning.'

She couldn't counter him with poems again.

He looked so determined. She would have to think of something.

A walk?

'All right then,' she said.

But he'd have to change first. She went back with him. While he was in his room, she shoved all the things she had wanted to take to Maxim hastily under the eiderdown and stuffed a pullover into her rucksack along with her rubber boots down in the hall. She waited for him in front of the house. He came with his air rifle. She was shocked. He seemed to be serious.

Silently they crossed the bridge and trudged through the trees on the slope. Anna noticed that Felix was watching her. When they came to a crossing, she said as lightly as possible:

'Let's cross over there.'

'Why do you want to go somewhere different from usual today?' asked Felix. 'Your tracks lead straight up here. I'm happy to go along with what you usually do.'

He must have thought up that sentence quite a while ago.

'If you like,' she said. 'But I don't always go the same way.'

They crossed two or three other paths. He was tenaciously following her tracks from the previous week, which were only faint, but still visible. The only tracks, it seemed, on this slope.

'I saw you pinch a roll in the Lamb yesterday,' he said.

'True,' she answered calmly, as her pulse began to race. 'I was hungry. Anything else?'

'I didn't see when you ate it,' he pressed on. 'You put it in your pocket.'

'You don't see a lot of things I do,' she said as peaceably as possible. 'And I don't see everything that *you* do. It's just as well really – isn't it?'

As they reached the place from which they could see

the bunker entrance, she went weak at the knees. You could clearly see her tracks disappearing into the bunker.

'So, do you always go to the bunker?' he asked.

'Not always, but often. Do you want to know where?'

He nodded and took his air rifle in his hands ready to shoot.

Of course it was only an air rifle. But if he aimed at someone's head, at the eyes! And he had proved to her at length what a good shot he was!

'You're making me nervous with that thing,' she said. 'What if it goes off by mistake!'

He just laughed and pointed the barrel at the ground.

She led him to her den with firm steps.

'I often sit there,' she said, 'even now in the winter, and write up the poems that come to me on the way. Quarter of an hour, half an hour, however long I can take the cold.'

He looked round, saw the table, the chair, the bunch of heather in the jam jar. She noticed how disappointed and embarrassed he was.

So long as he just doesn't ask about the notebook I write in, she thought nervously, and about the pen. She hadn't thought of that in the haste to repack her bag.

But the fear for Maxim worried her even more. He must be anxious about whether or not she was coming back. He had probably been waiting day and night for the last week for her knocking signal. Today was his Christmas Day. Wouldn't he be expecting her particularly today? Perhaps he was already standing in the main

125

corridor, assuming that she was alone, as always. If he came out now – unthinkable!

'I want to be a writer one day,' she whispered. 'But I've only told you. It's a secret I'm entrusting to you. Do you understand?'

Felix nodded and swallowed. 'Do you know what I thought?' he said with embarrassment. 'That you were hiding someone. Here in the bunker!'

'Good grief, what an imagination!' she laughed, feeling the blood rush to her face. Hastily she bent down and fiddled with her shoe. 'Who should I be hiding? An escaped convict? A spy? A deserter?'

'The eighth Russian,' he mumbled, so quietly she could hardly hear it. 'The one that didn't turn up again.' He looked at her uncertainly. 'You gave me the idea yourself: with the star and your wanderings and your opinions about Russians and with the book. I couldn't believe it. And didn't *want* to believe it! Because that's impossible: my sister – a traitor!' He lifted his head and breathed deeply. 'And so I simply had to prove to myself that my suspicion was rubbish. That's why I gave you such a grilling today.'

She laughed, more shrilly than she wanted. Perhaps in this situation it was wisest to make as much noise as possible, to warn Maxim of the danger.

'And what have you got in there, hey?' Felix asked suddenly, jumped behind her and pulled off the rucksack. She didn't stop him. He pulled out the pullover and boots, felt around in the empty bag, stuffed the pullover and boots back in without a word. Now he was bound to ask about the notebook and pen. She would react in surprise, embarrassment. Whoops – I've forgotten the most important things today! Though that would smack of a downright lie.

But he didn't ask.

'Finished?' she asked calmly.

She felt how mortified he was by this embarrassment.

'Forgive me,' he mumbled shamefacedly. 'I think I'm going mad. Let's go.'

All the way home he tried to be friendly to her again, showed her with every gesture, every word, that he was sorry for his suspicions. Poor Felix. How right he had been! But she must exploit his remorse as long as it lasted.

'You really have no idea,' she said with mild consideration, 'what it's like when you're writing a poem. The inspiration comes when it wants, sometimes even at night. Then you have to make sure you write it down before you forget. And you can't pin it down everywhere. Over there in the bunker, where I'm all alone and the forest rustles outside, that's the best place.'

He nodded.

That had gone quite well. But all the same, she hadn't been to Maxim. Today was his Christmas. She would have to find a way!

Towards the evening, as business was busiest in the Lamb, she helped for a while and then slipped away. She would have to hurry if she wanted to be back again before Mother came home. Felix had gone to see Donar in Uncle Franz's barn. The puppy still needed the milk and warmth of its mother, who had made a den there. And Grandmother could only think of Seff, because there was still no post from him.

Anna didn't even need to go home to fetch the rucksack. She had hidden it under the bridge. She found the way up the slope without difficulty, even in the dark. It was a moonlit night. The trees cast shadows, the snow glittered faintly.

She knocked, Maxim came towards her beaming with joy, he hugged her impetuously. She was so surprised that she forgot to pull away. But he soon drew back himself, serious again.

'*Danke*, Yeva.'

He took the rucksack from her and lit the way in front of them. She saw that he had stuck a candle to the concrete floor of one of the rooms, which was dark even in the daytime, and lit it. The sleeping bag lay next to it.

He dragged a small block of concrete over to it and laid the sofa cushion on top. Anna was glad. Maxim had himself under control again. She watched him surreptitiously. Since she had first met him, he had grown a proper beard. That made him seem older. The wound on his forehead had scabbed over. The injuries to his knuckles were healing too.

She unpacked the rucksack. He didn't pounce on the biscuits, the bread, the apples. He sat cross-legged on the sleeping bag, with the coat around his shoulders, looking at her. He must see her face just as she saw his, shimmering and casting shadows in the candlelight.

And then she pulled out the big map hesitantly, unfolded

it and spread it out between him and the candles. She saw how enthralled he was by the map. He stood up and fetched all his candles. Five stumps of different lengths. He also found a half-rotten board, put two pieces of rubble underneath it, lit the candle ends and stuck them to the wood. He took the candle standing on the floor in his hand.

Anna knelt on the sofa cushion. The map was now in the light. She pointed to the centre point of her world: the approximate location of the bunker.

That was by no means easy. Stiegnitz wasn't marked on this map. Not even Schonberg, which, after all, was more than ten times bigger than Stiegnitz. But the stream was there, on the banks of which she had discovered his trail, the stream which became a river further to the southwest. Somewhere around this bend, in the middle of the mountains.

Maxim bent over the map – so close that he almost touched it. Was he shortsighted? Had he previously worn glasses? Anna thought of her friend Sonja. She was very shortsighted and wore thick lenses. Without her glasses, if anything was a little way away from her, she could only make out its outline. And if she wanted to read something without the lenses, she practically had to crawl into the book. Without glasses she wouldn't be able to read a signpost, would stumble over branches in the forest, she wouldn't be able to tell whether something moving in a meadow at a distance was a cow or a deer.

Someone with such an impairment could only make his escape if he was accompanied by other people with good sight.

Perhaps *that* was the reason that Maxim didn't dare to flee to the Czech area?

Now he had looked enough, now Maxim knew the Here as well as the Now. But before Anna could reach for the flags, he stood up and fetched over the hiking map. He spread it out and shrugged his shoulders.

Of course! Why hadn't she thought of that? He didn't even know the name of the village where he had hidden and which she had led him out from! And he probably couldn't read the German letters!

She showed him Stiegnitz, she showed him the bunker. Even that was marked on the hiking map. Maxim made a mark here with his fingernail, an impression in the paper. And he put the two maps together hastily and once again bent over Europe. It was clear to her what he wanted to know now.

Slowly she stuck in one flag after another. In the meantime she had learned fairly precisely where the Russians, the British and the Americans stood. Every hole in the paper was bitter to her. She thought, that's what a soldier must feel when he's forced to raise his hands. Even though she had joined Grandmother on New Year's Eve in calling for the war finally to be over.

But that had just been family. Now she had the feeling of giving herself up through the position of the flags, of admitting the defeat to Maxim, the approaching end of the war that would be so humiliating for Germany.

She saw how amazed he was. He seemed to have totally forgotten that he was kneeling on the cold concrete. He kept shaking his head in disbelief. He had probably learnt nothing about where the fronts ran since he had been taken prisoner, so the flags must have been almost shockingly hopeful!

He took a deep breath, looked up and met her eyes. What meant hope for him, was a reason for fear in her. Fear of fighting in Stiegnitz, of the destruction of the village, of the revenge of the Czechs, of humiliation and atrocities. Fear of seeing the people close to her suffer, yes even of losing them, fear of her own death.

Anna forced herself to think of the second present that she had brought: a big box full of brightly coloured chalk. She pointed to the walls. Such an unending amount of space for writing and drawing! He nodded, reached for a piece of white chalk, stood up and – the candle in his other hand – sketched a bird on the wall; it looked like a plucked sparrow. And one leg was much longer than the other. But when Maxim drew a branch in its beak and said '*Mir*', she knew what he wanted to tell her. She nodded. He made an expansive gesture over the map and said: '*Mir*, Yeva, *Mir*.'

Yes, peace for all. And peace soon!

Before Anna went, she handed him a calendar for the new year and showed him that she would come again in a week. And she took the time to make it clear to him that if in the future she knocked twice in a row in the corridor then it was all clear. But if she only knocked once then he was in danger. Then he shouldn't show himself.

He looked at her uneasily and tried to tell from her face whether anyone was on his trail. But she indicated no. It was her brother. She tried to draw, to explain. He probably only understood that she was talking about a child.

'*Auf wiedersehen*,' she said in parting. He answered. It sounded like '*Do svidanija*, Yeva.'

Do svidanija. That sounded nice. It had rhythm.

13

The holidays were over, Anna had to leave. Until now she had always looked forward to the beginning of term. To be in Schonberg – out there in the real world!

This time she departed with a heavy heart. Her thoughts were half with Maxim, half with Seff. Where could she get food for Maxim? There still hadn't been any post from Seff. And a Russian offensive had begun – according to the latest reports – on the Vistula and the border with East Prussia. The Soviet army had mobilised to conquer East Prussia and the Warthegau. That meant that the Eastern Front was now already on German soil!

In Schonberg station, refugees from East Prussia were being cared for by Red Cross nurses on their journey into the Protectorate. A hospital train stood at the next platform. A wounded soldier was screaming. It sounded horrible. Anna put her fingers in her ears and left the station as quickly as she could.

Refugees, fleeing the Eastern Front, were being forcibly billeted in Schonberg. Even with Gisela Beranek. An elderly woman from East Prussia was staying in her bedroom, who, according to Gisela, still had no idea what had happened to her.

'It all fitted,' whispered Anna to Gisela. 'He's well.'

Gisela came with her up to the attic and said, after shutting the door behind them: 'It would be better not to talk about him downstairs any more. The old lady is incredibly nosy. And I won't get rid of her until the war's over.'

Anna nodded. 'And when do you think it'll be over?' she asked nervously.

'By Easter at the latest.' Gisela lowered her voice even more and continued: 'You can bet on that. All that matters now is whether we survive the End, into the peace. No easy task, I'm afraid. So far we're OK. So far, the world is falling to bits elsewhere. But in a couple of weeks, it'll be here too.'

Anna buried her face in her hands and groaned: 'I'm so afraid!'

'*You'll* be well off then, though,' whispered Gisela, stroking her arm. 'With the man that you're helping. When the war's over, the others will have the say. But don't let yourself be caught before then! You know my views. I owe them to my husband, because they forced him to become a soldier. I'll carry on helping you with this business. But always remember: It's not just your life that you're risking, but mine too. And I don't really want to die yet. I'm curious about what life after the war will be like. About life in peace. And I'm looking forward to being able to open my mouth again.'

Anna nodded, her eyes wide.

'Believe me,' said Gisela, 'your *protégé* has already cost me sleepless nights. The whole thing is stupidly risky. I feel as if I'm sitting on a ticking bomb!'

But Anna took hope and comfort from this conversation. With such a good friend, she would manage it.

*

A gloomy mood reigned in Schonberg. In Bossel, only a few kilometres away, a training camp barracks had been blown up. Sabotage. Fourteen- and fifteen-year-olds had been taking part in a course: handling Bazookas. The explosion had torn six boys apart and seriously injured more than twenty.

Anna was occupied by many questions now, to which she had no answers. How could the Czech, who had destroyed the bunker and caused the deaths of those six boys, live with his guilt? And then the policemen who had chased the escaped Russians: how did they deal with being ordered to shoot unarmed men? And Father? Would he have raised his arm in the Hitler salute?

And why, why on earth, was there practically no resistance from all the parents, against what the propaganda, the state education, was doing to their children? After all, Felix was not the only fanatic!

At school Anna's distraction was hardly noticeable any longer. Nobody was on top of things now. People whispered the latest news and rumours to each other in the breaks. Sonja, who sat next to her, had something so awful to report, that Anna shook her head distraught. That *couldn't* be true! They were whispering very quietly out in the corridor where there was a lot of noise. Sonja knew that Anna would keep her mouth shut. To tell her something like this was dangerous. In Poland thousands of Jews, women and children too, had been killed by the Germans. In quarries. Her brother had told her, and he'd apparently belonged to such a firing squad himself. And another comrade was supposed to have been reliably informed by a railway worker that there were camps of Jews, into which whole trainloads disappeared. If everyone that they had taken there was still alive, then these camps would be enormous, like whole cities. But they weren't. They always stayed just as small...

It was bold to tell her that. Anna knew. A man from Mellersdorf who had repeated similar rumours had been taken away and never came back. And Gisela had told her about a woman who had ended up in prison because she had spread it around that they were killing all the mentally ill.

If they were really *German* firing squads, *German* camps and trains, then the same atrocities were being committed on the German side as by the Russians! Perhaps even worse? Did the League *Führerinnen* know that, the teachers, Mother and Uncle Franz? What would Felix say about that if he heard it? She shrugged. He would have an explanation ready for everything. 'You can't make an omelette without breaking eggs' or even, 'That's part of the purification of the race'. And Seff? Did he know about it? Or had he, if the quarry story was even true, in the end... himself...

Seff. Perhaps he wasn't even alive any more.

Never, since the war had begun, had there been so many death notices. Her piano teacher's son was dead too, and the dentist on the corner, almost at the same time as his son, and the nice blond postman and Sonja's brother and two cousins of her classmate who sat behind her.

Once when she got to her attic after school, an old zinc bucket was standing there, next to a dented lead bowl. In it there was an everyday towel, the sort you used to be able to get in every store, wrapped around a piece of everyday soap, as well as a comb and toothbrush. Next to that in another bag were a couple of cooked potatoes and half a loaf of bread. And something very special: a bar of chocolate. That must have come from Holland, where Herr Beranek had been stationed for a whole year.

All for Maxim.

Anna was ashamed. Why hadn't she thought of a towel and soap, comb and toothbrush? How could she have forgotten that a man doesn't just need warmth and nourishment to survive, but also cleanliness! Even if it was only so as not to lose his self respect.

She covered the bucket with the lead bowl and bound them securely.

Before she travelled home on Saturday, she rolled up her extra duvet and stuffed it in her rucksack, after carefully checking for any nametags. She removed the company label. She would get through the winter even without this woollen under layer. The coldest days of the winter were still to come. At least Maxim wouldn't freeze, even if he couldn't be full. And she wasn't stealing the duvet. She had been given it by Grandmother a couple of years ago, as part of her bottom drawer.

She skipped the League sports again. Now that the war was on their own front doorstep, people must have more important things to do than to tell her off because she'd skived a few times.

By the time she boarded the train, the contents of the bucket had increased. She had bought a few more things on her ration card. And once again this week, she hadn't been full herself.

Only a young soldier, hardly twenty years old, was sitting in her compartment. He had opened the window. As Anna sat down opposite him, she noticed that he smelled of alcohol. He had an arm missing and his right eye was heavily bandaged.

She looked surreptitiously at the one hanging sleeve of his uniform jacket. How awful. And the man was so young! As he noticed her look, he took a swig from his bottle and mumbled something. Anna looked away quickly, she was ashamed and felt herself going red.

But then, quite unexpectedly, he began to talk, haltingly and with a slurred voice. He had stumbled into an ambush by Russian partisans, he told her. Near Kiev. And he had been lucky again. Thirteen of his comrades had been killed in the assault, some of them in the most dreadful ways.

'But we...didn't spare...any...if we could...catch them', he said. 'I was there...when a...girl was...was hanged.' Anna jumped. 'She still...looked...scarcely more than...more than a...child. Just...because she...wanted to take the...parti...sans some food. And...because she didn't...want to give away... where they were...hiding.' He leaned back. 'You can...believe me...I've had...enough of...it.' She was reminded of what Sonja had told her a few days ago. Did she dare to ask the man about it?

'Is it really true,' she asked, almost whispering, 'that in Poland...in quarries, thousands of Jews...'

'Be...careful,' he said and lowered his voice in the same way. 'A question...like that...these days...can cost...you your life...After all...you don't know me...at all.'

Anna felt the blood pounding in her temples.

He bent forward. His boozy breath struck her in the face.

'I *have* heard...of it,' he said. 'The army...has a hand in...that too...The havoc the lads...sometimes wrought...in Russia...' Slowly he leant back, took a deep draught from his bottle and stayed silent for a while.

Then he suddenly looked Anna in the face. 'The... girl...who they...hanged...' he said, 'she didn't... look any different...from our girls...The bast...'

Then a guard opened the compartment door. No sooner had he gone again, than the train stopped. Mellersdorf.

'Be careful,' he whispered after her.

'Thank you,' she whispered back.

'Is that you, Anna?' asked a woman from Stiegnitz, who was going the same way. 'Then we can walk together...'

But Anna turned off at the end of Mellersdorf, to the bridge. She had something to do in the farm there.

So she really had to turn into the farm, because the woman was peering at her curiously from the path. She knew Mother and would tell her that she had met Anna.

The two old people who owned the farm had lost their only son two or three years ago. Fallen in Russia. Anna always saw a few sheep grazing at the side of their field. She would ask about a sheepskin.

Of course they didn't have one – at least not for her. But the old woman gave her two apples. Something else for Maxim! Although she would have liked to have bitten into the juicy fruit herself. She stayed and talked with the old couple for a while longer.

As she left the farm, the woman from Stiegnitz was no longer to be seen. And Anna had lost a lot of time.

Once again Maxim was waiting for her deep in the corridor with his quiet '*Dobro pozhalovat*', his welcome, and led her to his rooms. He didn't fall on the chocolate, as he had done with the *Blutwurst* that time, although even now he couldn't be really full. But he reached for the soap, comb and toothbrush, with a quiet, joyful exclamation. And he took the duvet with an almost ceremonial movement.

'*Danke, danke!*'

After she had unpacked everything and he had grasped that the bucket and bowl should stay here too, he led her into his brightest room, the one with the hole in the ceiling. Proudly he demonstrated to her the calendar system that he had drawn on the wall. The Sundays he had ringed in red. And the map lay spread out on the floor.

Anna moved almost all the flags. Ever nearer, ever nearer.

The pins that she had to stick into the paper in the middle of East Prussia and between Aachen and the Rhine caused her almost physical pain.

When she wanted to set off, he led her to the calendar wall again. He took a piece of chalk and drew a pair of glasses. Then he pointed to his eyes. He gestured up to the hole in the roof, pulled down the corners of his mouth, shook his head. Then he held both his hands in front of him like an open book, right up close to him. Anna understood. Now it was conclusively clear to her why he hadn't left the bunker – despite his new clothes and his better physical condition. Maxim was extremely shortsighted. He *couldn't* find his way out there. He needed glasses.

She wanted to talk about it with Gisela. After all, her husband had been an optician. Perhaps he had kept a few pairs of glasses? Perhaps they included some which would be helpful.

She arrived home just half an hour late.

But the news which greeted her had distracted Grandmother's attention: Seff had written! It said in his letter that he hadn't got round to writing lately. They had been transferred several times. And would Mother send him the photo of Father, he had a picture of everyone except him.

Mother already knew that Anna had gone into the Langers' farm.

She had asked about a sheepskin there? She laughed. 'You could have spared yourself the effort. They don't

141

turn anything out, store everything up for even worse times. They're well known for it. What do you want with a sheepskin anyway?'

Anna was ready for that question. All the same, she must always watch out, be on her guard. That wore her down. Always lying, lying, lying – and remembering the lies carefully. If just one link in the chain didn't fit, it would cause suspicion.

'It would be nice by my bed,' she said.

Mother shook her head. 'What ideas! In times like these! The rest of us are thinking about what the Russians will do here...' She broke off, coughed and then continued: 'And you're dreaming of a bedside rug!'

Felix pulled Anna away. She must admire his skill at shooting. Now he was shooting right across the yard from the house door to the barn wall: almost twice as far as at Christmas. But he was still hitting the target almost as well.

'If only shooting was a subject at school!' he cried, as Anna watched in astonishment. 'Then I'd get at least one One!'

Poor Felix. He really didn't do well at school. That was why he hadn't been able to follow Anna to Schonberg. But he was a great help to Mother in the Lamb. Indispensable.

'What would I do without you?' she said often. And she really meant it.

Felix was now always very friendly to Anna. Just once was there a heated exchange between them, when he came home with the news that Czech saboteurs had wanted to blow up the railway line between Glatz and Brünn, but been caught.

'They should be strung up from the closest tree!' he shouted.

'If you were Czech,' she said, 'you'd think what they'd done was good.'

'If I were Czech,' he answered, 'I would try everything to become more German. Because we are the Master Race, chosen to lead the other races!'

'Chosen, by *whom*?'

'By Providence.'

'And who says that?'

'The *Führer*, who else?' answered Felix like a shot. 'And he's always right!'

Anna saw Grandmother cross herself, bent over the stove, and couldn't stop herself from saying: 'That's what you think. But thinking isn't knowing. And Hitler is just a man, who can make mistakes.'

Felix rushed on Anna with clenched fists and shouted in her face: 'Have you taken it on yourself to destroy my faith? Do you want to weaken me? You're unreliable! Totally and utterly unreliable! That's practically treason!'

'Stop it,' Grandmother interrupted them. 'You're brother and sister, aren't you?'

'If you weren't my sister,' he said stonily, 'I'd probably denounce you – for undermining military morale.'

'Jesus, Mary and Joseph!' cried Grandmother, storming over and boxing Felix's ears. 'Anyone would think the devil had got into you! Denounce her for something like that!'

143

'You too!' he screamed at her.

So she brewed him some St John's wort tea. It had, she said, a calming effect. In fact, it was good for anything.

But Felix didn't touch it.

14

Anna was pleased to see that the days were gradually getting longer. She no longer arrived home on Saturdays in the dark, but in the twilight. And when she arrived in Schonberg on Sunday evenings it was still halfway light.

She spoke to Gisela about Maxim's shortsightedness. No, her husband hadn't kept anything from the business at home. But he had been shortsighted himself. Gisela could give her a pair of his discarded glasses. Perhaps the lenses would suit him, to some extent at least.

Anna took the glasses with her and Maxim tried them when she next visited the bunker, full of joy and hope. But he shook his head disappointedly.

Anna had now developed a method of obtaining food without stealing. From week to week she let Grandmother pack up more food before she left for Schonberg. She was always hungry there. And think of poor Gisela Beranek. She only had her ration card and nothing else. Gisela was always so nice to her, although she had quite enough of her own worries. And so on.

Grandmother believed it all and gave her things. And it was really true. Most people did much better here in the village than in town. Of course, farmers had to hand over practically all their harvest, but they still had enough for themselves. There was even enough left over for them to help out their relatives and friends.

'Oh yes, put a lot of sauerkraut in!' Anna said to Grandmother. 'It's good for you. And Gisela particularly likes your sauerkraut!'

She felt that she was being really crafty. Gisela would get none of the sauerkraut. That found its way, with her permission, into the bunker. It didn't need to be cooked. There was a proper system of exchange between them. Gisela accepted anything from Anna's shopping bag which needed cooking: potatoes, flour, wholemeal. In exchange she gave away things that could be eaten raw: oat flakes, bread, bacon rinds and an occasional kipper.

She also donated two pairs of long johns and a thick woollen vest that her husband had worn on climbing trips to the mountains.

And a pair of ankle length house shoes left by her father-in-law turned up too. She had discovered them, covered in cobwebs, in the cellar.

And another pair of glasses. Also left by her father-in-law. Anna put them on and saw nothing but blurred colours and shapes. She was filled with new hope. But on her next journey home, a fat man accidentally sat on her bag. As he got up again, she looked for them hurriedly and put her hand into nothing but shards of glass.

At the end of January, as Anna was eating her stew in the school canteen, her *Führerin* appeared, the one who led the Saturday sports lessons. A girl hardly older than herself.

Darkly she demanded an explanation from Anna. She had missed week after week now. It couldn't continue!

Anna asked for patience. She had sprained her ankle. But as soon as she had stopped limping, she'd be there. And she left the rest of her stew and limped away.

'I'm expecting a doctor's note – and soon!' the girl called after her.

And all this time, the Russians were already in Elbing, had long ago crossed the Vistula, reached the Oder, overrun Upper Silesia.

Masses of refugees from East Prussia, which was now encircled, were trying to escape across the Baltic in every possible available ship. Countless columns of refugees were approaching on every road out of the east. But in Schonberg and Stiegnitz, everything was still as ever, and you weren't allowed to skip League sports!

And it wasn't just the *Führerin* who was causing Anna to worry. Things were often very precarious at home too.

'Is it true that you never come straight home from the station, but wander around in the forest somewhere?' asked Grandmother, as Anna arrived home on a Saturday in February, rather tired. She had been late leaving the bunker and had run down the slope.

Felix, who was involved in brooding over his homework, raised his head and looked at her expectantly.

'Yes,' she answered lightly. 'Sometimes. The forest is so beautiful in the winter. And at the end of a school week like this I'm gasping for fresh air. For freedom of movement most of all. Working late on my homework every evening . . . I get so stiff! After all, grammar school is quite different from the school here!'

That was a good argument. Grandmother would take her word for it. But she didn't let go. 'With all your luggage?'

'Never heard of a pack march?' countered Anna.

'We go on pack marches too,' said Felix.

Anna threw him a grateful glance. 'I still want to be physically fit, even if I'm not a boy,' she said.

But Grandmother was stubborn: 'There's forest behind our farm too.'

'But the view here isn't nearly as good as over there on the slope.'

'That's right,' said Felix. 'You can see the whole valley from there.'

'But didn't you always have sport on Saturday afternoons?'

'It's been moved to Friday.'

Now Grandmother let slip what was really bothering her: 'Tell me the truth, are you meeting someone in the forest?'

Anna felt herself going red. She began to laugh. She doubled up with laughter. You could go red from laughter too. Felix laughed with her.

'Who would she be meeting?' he cried. 'Everyone her age has gone. There's only Wenzel Krause left.' He turned to Anna. 'You're not seeing him by any chance?'

Then Grandmother had to laugh too. 'Ah, the youth of today,' she sighed. 'When I was young, girls couldn't just wander around the forest like that, all alone. That would soon have got you a bad reputation.'

That closed the subject. But Anna's knees were still

trembling. While she was extremely relieved that Grandmother had suspected something quite different, utterly ridiculous, she was equally discomfited by Felix's behaviour. How did he know that she had met Wenzel Krause?

As soon as he had taken his school stuff up to his room, she ran after him and, after shutting the door behind them, took him to task. 'Have you been spying on me?'

He looked at her in astonishment. 'I happened to look out of the window as you came up the slope,' he said. 'So I saw that he was standing at the bottom and watching you. That's why I thought of him when Grandmother started asking you all those silly questions. That's all.'

A couple of weeks ago his look would have convinced her of his honesty. Rock solid. But having learned to lie so well herself lately – why shouldn't he too be capable of lying with the most honest face in the world?

The first German test of the new year made Anna really alert. The topic was DULCE ET DECORUM EST PRO PATRIA MORI. That meant: It is lovely and honourable to die for one's country.

There was a great deal to say about that. On no account did she want to get out of answering this time, even if she didn't feel properly rested. She thought about all the people she knew who had fallen; about the six boys who'd been blown up with their barracks; about the Czech waiter from the Café Paris; about the young girl on the gallows who'd helped the partisans and about the seven Russians who'd been shot on the run. She thought about Felix too. If he were taking this test, then, young as he was, he'd probably get a better mark than her. Because his lines would shine with enthusiasm. Wasn't his favourite line in his favourite song: 'O Germany we devote to you our death, the smallest deed. For once he greets our ranks, we become the greatest seed!' Such enthusiasm, such devotion would certainly greatly benefit the overall assessment of the essay.

Her essay was a tapestry of ifs and buts, agreement and reservations, and in the closing sentence she once more summed up all her thoughts: I believe that it is at least as honourable, and certainly lovelier, to live for one's country!

She underlined the word live three times.

As the bell rang, she hesitated for a moment. She could still tear up the essay, hide it, just not give it in. But she shut her exercise book and gave it to the teacher. Come what may, she would accept it. The grandfathers and *Pimpfe* were already blockading the entrances to the villages and towns. And the old lady from East Prussia had received a letter from relatives in Neisse that said they could hear the sound of artillery from there. How far away was Neisse? Hardly more than a hundred kilometres.

And every Saturday Anna made her way up to the bunker and provided Maxim with provisions, batteries, candles. Every time she arrived, his face filled with hope. But after she had unpacked, his face seemed disappointed. Wasn't he happy with the food?

He saw what she was wondering. So he held both his thumbs and index fingers to his eyes like circles. Then he pointed to the map and tried to explain something.

So it was glasses he had been hoping for so badly. And that he would finally be able to leave the bunker. Anna could only shrug her shoulders regretfully.

She had got to know Maxim rather better by now. She had found out that he was twenty-four. And that he could play chess. He had drawn a chessboard on the floor, with stones marked with chalk laid out as figures. Once he invited her to play. She didn't decline his request, but in the middle of the game she wanted to break off to go home. But he had already won by then anyway.

There were some things about him which repulsed her: when he was embarrassed he pulled hairs from his moustache into his mouth with his lower lip and chewed on them. If she didn't understand what he meant straight away, he clicked his fingers. And the thing that bothered her the most: he blew his nose with his hand. That made her stomach heave.

But he had no handkerchiefs. What else should he use to wipe his nose? And she probably had habits that got on his nerves too.

There were also things about him that she particularly liked. Such as when he sat opposite her humming a song, and his whole upper body swayed. It was a shame that she couldn't ask him to sing out loud. She was touched by his little sketches, which he finished eagerly once she had brought him a sketchpad, pencils, sharpeners and rubbers. Roots, his camp, his hand – he tried to draw everything. Even a beetle – making a great effort to capture the gleam of the shell on its back. Here he had almost rubbed through the paper.

She saw his fingernails. The next time she brought him her nail scissors.

Once he had shocked her by first unwrapping the scarf from his neck, in her presence, then removing not only his pullover, but also his shirt. She had drawn back but he had reassured her with gestures, then raised his arm and shown her a boil.

Gisela gave her some salve for Maxim. That helped.

Anna never forgot to reposition the flags on the map every Saturday. Not even after the dreadful bombing raid on Dresden, which killed thousands of women and children.

In Schonberg, all the schools were shut at the end of February. The Russians had already reached Breslau. And if the armies broke through from there, how were the many pupils, whose families lived a fair distance from Schonberg, to get home safely? As well as this, they needed the school buildings to set up field hospitals in them. Because there were ever increasing numbers of wounded soldiers to be accommodated.

School was over. Now she wouldn't get a mark for the German test. Where would the exercise book end up? Perhaps on the school roof. Perhaps in a teacher's dustbin. Perhaps among the flames as Schonberg burned.

No more evening meetings, no League sports. No more reprimands from the *Führerin* for skiving her duties. Unlimited holidays. And yet it was no reason to rejoice. Anna went home dejectedly. On the same day that she left Schonberg, a family of three from Silesia were billeted in the attic.

As a goodbye present, Anna gave the little jack-in-the-box to Gisela after all. The times had now become so threatening, that you could only get through with humour. If you could dredge any up. Gisela had to laugh as the little box opened. That was something, anyway.

Now Anna would have to see how she would manage on her own.

Without Gisela.

15

So now Anna was cut off from Schonberg for an indefinite period, was back at home in her hole, far from the real world. Three months ago she would have rebelled, done all that was humanly possible to be allowed to stay in Schonberg. But now she saw this change differently. And not only that, but many, many other things too. It seemed that she had also changed outwardly. When Anna visited Aunt Agnes, she cried: 'You've got so thin, child. And you've grown so much too!' And the new postmistress, who came from higher up in the mountains and didn't know Anna, addressed her as an adult.

Now Anna could no longer barricade herself in her bedroom whenever she felt like it. She saw the way Mother was slaving and Grandmother was helping out in the Lamb, although her back was giving her ever more trouble. And Felix spent the whole day working in the guest rooms, apart from when he was at school or doing Hitler Youth service.

So she helped in the Lamb too, from morning to evening, wherever help was needed. She peeled potatoes, lent Hedi a hand, buttered bread for the French prisoners of war, shovelled snow or hacked wood, kept an eye on the pots on the stove, helped to clean the dining room and the kitchen, served the guests when

Felix couldn't cope on his own, did the shopping and sorted the ration card coupons.

Dreary activities. But she tried to make the best of them. She got up even before Grandmother in the mornings, made coffee, laid the table and, while she was doing this, listened to the radio programme which broadcast the names of executed Czechs. There were women among them too. Even young girls, only a little older than Anna herself. Spies, saboteurs, partisans. Spanners in the German works.

'Turn that off,' Grandmother said once, appearing in the kitchen a little earlier than usual. 'That's nothing to do with us...'

As soon as she arrived in the Lamb, Anna exploited every opportunity to gather food. She almost always wore her trousers and the baggy jumper. That had already paid off. There was even room for a pot full of food in the trouser pockets. Admittedly, if it was full to the brim, Anna had to wear a belt to hold the trousers up...

Now as well as slices of bread, she could swipe left-over dumplings which were still swimming in the pots. If they were too big to go in the pot, she forced them in. She also took half dumplings and crumbs. *Every little helps*, as it said, embroidered in cross-stitch, on one of Grandmother's cushions.

She collected anything, everything, in this pot: boiled potatoes, fried potatoes, dregs from soup plates, remains of vegetables, sauces and puddings, burnt rice, with the whole lot often mixed together. However it tasted, it must still be better than dogs and rats.

She felt like the king's daughter in the Grimm fairy tale, who had to work as a kitchen maid, helping the castle cook – without payment, just for free food. She had fixed a little pot in each of the pockets of her skirt, in which she used to take home 'her share of the leavings'. Until the whole lot fell out when King Thrushbeard danced with her.

She now often spent time with Aunt Agnes and Uncle Franz. Every day there was a trough full of cooked potatoes for the pigs. Only tiny potatoes, some of them no bigger than marbles. And in their skins.

'Would you mind,' she said to Aunt Agnes, 'if I took some of these potatoes home for our rabbits now and then? How else are they supposed to fatten up this winter?'

Aunt Agnes was the best natured and most innocent woman in the world. She didn't mind. 'No, no, you take them, Anna!'

Now and then, Anna really stuck a couple of the potatoes into the rabbits' hutch, so that it was all fair.

One day a card came from Gisela. She was well, the people in the attic were nice, the woman from East Prussia got nosier every day, she poked her nose in everywhere. And scribbled in tiny letters on the side: 'I hope that all is well with you, as it should be. Best wishes, Gisela.'

The very next day, Anna wrote back: she was now helping in the Lamb for whole days and wasn't letting any leftovers get away. Her uncle cooked up his smallest potatoes for the pigs and she sometimes nibbled on them. And everyone, everyone, was well and cheerful. Gisela would be sure to know what she meant by that.

Once more the rumours in Stiegnitz revolved around Hedi, who carried out her work at the Lamb looking pale and wrapped in thought. Sometimes her eyes were red with crying. People said lately that it had been one of the French prisoners of war. One of them had been seen slipping out of Hedi's cottage very early in the morning. It stood right next to the old factory where the Frenchmen were housed.

Before she spoke about it, Mother made sure that Felix wasn't there.

'If anyone asks me about it,' she said, 'I don't know anything.' Then she turned to Grandmother: 'And you don't know anything either. Do you understand me, Mother?'

Grandmother made a strained face, bent over the stove, and stirred busily.

'So long as it doesn't get through to people who'll make an affair of state out of it,' sighed Mother. 'They're capable of refusing to grant me any more Frenchmen. And what will I do without Hedi?'

After a while, she added, still annoyed: 'How could she have been so stupid!'

That made Anna think.

'But what if she loved him?' she asked.

'She knew very well that she was risking a severe punishment if she, a German, carried on with a French prisoner of war!' grumbled Mother.

'But what if she loved him?' repeated Anna.

Then Mother suddenly went very quiet.

When Anna came home tired late in the evening, she still sometimes tried to scribble some kind of poem in an exercise book. After all, Felix might want to see what she was always writing. He understood next to nothing about it, but what she wrote, page by page in the book still had to be a bit poem-like. Drowsily she rhymed: 'Bones aching, heart pounding/All the world in flames/Snow falling, bells sounding/No more time for games!'

Felix. It was hardly any time since he had been her sweet little baby brother. Now she no longer trusted him. Now she considered him to be dangerous. Was he watching her? Was he snuffling around after her again? Or was she just imagining all that? Was she already suffering from a persecution complex?

She had succeeded *once* in allaying his suspicions. Another time he wouldn't just take her word for it like that!

Over in the boys' room, Donar, Felix's dog, whined every evening. Already half asleep, she shoved the exercise book behind the other books on her shelf. Her other poetry book lay there too, actually an autograph book, bound in satin. That was where she had written that summer, two and a half years ago, in her den in the bunker. But Felix wasn't to set eyes on that book. She had written a lot about love – true love, the way she had imagined it then. She still thought that some of those poems were good. Felix would be bound to make fun of them.

But he took stuff about 'German Stock/as a Rock', where 'Brave Banners Wave' seriously. You could see the way his heart swelled then! Doubts? Not for him. For him, everything was clear.

He had been over the moon since the Hitler Youth had been learning to shoot with real weapons. He was the best shot! Whenever he was with Anna for a while, he painted her an enthusiastic picture of the way he would defend Stiegnitz as a member of the *Volkssturm*.

'To the last drop of blood,' Anna allowed herself to say once. Then he looked at her sideways, suspicious. Was she making fun of him?

'Of course,' he said defiantly. 'For *Führer*, People and Fatherland.'

Anna remembered how he had stormed enthusiastically into the Lamb with news: 'Tomorrow we start building barricades here! It says so on the blackboard. And I'm joining in!'

'Your voice hasn't even broken yet!' Mother had shouted at him.

But at the beginning of March he had turned fourteen and was now old enough to join the *Volkssturm*.

In Stiegnitz too the school was closed now. You fell over children everywhere, even in the Lamb. The older ones probably had to help out at home. But the younger kids swarmed around the village. There were even the tracks of two children heading up the slope to the Moserwald, as Anna was shocked to discover. But she was relieved to see that they hadn't gone near the entrance to the bunker. The dark entrance hole must have seemed too creepy for the children.

All this time, Maxim was very quiet whenever Anna arrived, even quieter than usual, and didn't show what he felt as she repositioned the flags: in Remagen and Cologne, in front of the Austrian border, by Danzig. He never forgot his '*Dobro pozhalovat*' when she arrived or his '*Danke*' when she left again. And, heaven knew how he managed it, he always returned the cooking pot to her clean.

Now, after she had brought him another packet of chalk, he had also filled the walls of the second half-lit room with drawings – of flowers and animals, patterns and spirals.

Anna worked it out. He had now been in the bunker for over three months, and, apart from her short visits, always alone. Alone with his fear, his probably unpleasant memories, his longings. She pondered. How could she help him to pass the time without leaving anything in the bunker which could betray her? She brought him dry wood for carving, brought him a sheet of sandpaper. And another box of chalk, which this time she'd bought in the city.

But the walls lit by daylight were already nearly full. She got hold of a rag, a scrap of sheet from Grandmother's sewing things, which would give nothing away. He used it to wash the walls down again and drew new things: the silhouette of a town; churches with opulent domed towers and ornate crosses; an island with palm trees. He pointed to the churches and said 'Kremlin', pointed to a city silhouette and said 'Leningrad'. But he remarked dismissively of the island, 'Fantasia'.

Fantasia. Another Russian word. A word which sounded quite similar in German and Russian.

She wondered what he did for a living. She pointed to him, drew a man driving a tractor on the wall and put a question mark next to it. When he didn't understand what she meant, she drew, in a colourful row, a man with a hammer, one with a chef's hat and spoon, a fireman with a hose, a violinist.

Then he nodded, grabbed another piece of chalk and drew, his face only a hand span away from the wall, a lot of figures, like stickmen, next to each other; all behind desks, and a bigger one in front of them, with a book. He pointed to the bigger one and then to himself. And to remove all doubt, he pointed to the many smaller stickmen and then held his hand out flat at different heights from the floor: one metre, one metre twenty, one metre thirty.

So he was a teacher. A primary school teacher. He pulled from his coat the photo that she already knew, pointed at his father and mother and drew a row of houses and letters on the wall and walked his index finger and middle finger like legs to each house. Postman and postwoman. And his older brother? Maxim drew a ship on the waves. Easy to understand. He was a sailor.

Anna bent over the map, guessed at various places in the Soviet Union, shrugged and looked at him. He pointed to Leningrad. Then he took the chalk again, indicated the photo, drew a cross and raised his shoulders. That could only mean one thing: he didn't know whether or not his family were still alive.

She tried to remember. Hadn't Leningrad been besieged for months by the German army? Perhaps the family were long dead – starved, frozen, crushed by rubble. And his brother must be a soldier.

Anna took the chalk from Maxim's hand and drew, with a few strokes, her father, her mother, Grandmother, Seff, herself and Felix. She sketched Grandmother with a crooked back and headscarf, she crossed Father out and drew a cross next to him. She pointed to Seff and then to the line of flags along the Russo-German Front. And next to Felix she wrote the number 14.

He nodded thoughtfully, then fetched the lead bowl full of water and washed her family picture away again, with his bare hand. She nodded sadly: those drawings could give her away. So he was thinking of her too.

'*Spassibo*,' she said quietly.

How much better he smelled since he'd had the soap!

16

One morning in the middle of March, Hedi failed to appear at the Lamb. It happened to be a day on which there was a particularly large amount of work ahead. Mother sent Anna over to find out what was wrong. Anna found the neighbours in a state of utter confusion: Hedi had been taken away a quarter of an hour ago – by a policeman and a man in plain clothes. A neighbour had watched her being brought out of the house.

'She was crying and called out, "What about the children, the children!" and wanted to run back into the house,' she reported. 'But then the plain clothes man slapped her and roared, "French whore!" and "You miserable bitch, getting involved with foreigners!" And the policeman growled: "The children will be sent to a home."' Horrified, Anna went back to the Lamb and told them what she had found out.

Mother was beside herself: 'Such a hard-working woman! I won't find anyone to replace her. What will I do now?' And then she forgot to be careful and complained: 'As if they didn't have more important things to do now than to bother about such small fry. While the whole world is going under around them, that poor thing is being barbarously punished because she slept with a Frenchman! But I'll tell you one thing: Hedi's children go into a home over my dead body!'

She ran over to see Uncle Franz. He telephoned around all over the place for a whole hour. But he managed it. Mother was granted the right to look after Hedi's children. But as far as Hedi herself was concerned, the authorities remained resolute. 'She has already admitted having been involved with one of the Frenchmen,' said Uncle Franz.

But she hadn't given away his name.

There were interrogations in the factory too. People in the village said that all eighty-six Frenchmen claimed to have slept with Hedi. So their rations for the next three Sundays had been cancelled. It wasn't only the French who laughed at this punishment, the villagers did too. Everyone knew that the farmers would give their prisoners supplies for the Sundays to take back to the camp. Corruption? The local police didn't appreciate extra work. They only bothered about orders 'from above'. Mother brought Hedi's children to stay at the Lamb, with the evacuated women from the Ruhr. They would manage somehow; after all, it wasn't forever. And in any case, Hedi's children would be better off here in the Lamb than in a home. Anna wandered around the whole time weak at the knees, and hardly any use for anything.

'Pull yourself together!' Mother snapped as she hurried over. 'It's not the first time that something like this has happened. Hedi will come back, a bit the worse for wear, of course. There's no death penalty for loving a Frenchman. If you're getting so worked up about something like this, what do you think of the business in

Mährisch-Ostrau? A woman there hid a Russian. They shot her on the spot as well when they dragged him out of hiding.'

The world went black before Anna's eyes. She leant against the wall.

'My God,' cried Mother, the next time she came over, 'you really need to get over your thin skin in times like this. How else are you going to survive?'

That evening Anna couldn't sleep. She tossed and turned and couldn't think clearly. Over in the boys' room Donar was whimpering.

No, no, she couldn't be shot!

She jumped up and ran barefoot in the cold over to Felix.

'Can't you get your damn dog to shut up?' she shouted. 'Do I have to listen to it whining all night?'

She ran back to her room, stuffed cotton wool in her ears, pulled her duvet over her head and prayed that the war would be over quickly. Another three months at the most, Gisela had said. But that was nearly up and a quick end was still not in sight. To be sure, the Americans were advancing in the south of Germany, but the British still hadn't been able to cross the Rhine, and the Russians had stopped at the Oder. Why wasn't it going faster?

She thought about Maxim. So long as he didn't have any glasses, he would have to stay in his hiding place. And she would have to slip up there at least once a week to take him provisions. If she went less often it would be less dangerous, but then she would risk the food that she collected for Maxim going off. Spring was coming, it was getting warmer, the leftovers from the Lamb, which she hid in stoneware pots in the hayloft, spoiled more and more quickly. And now that winter was over, you met people from the village again, in the fields, the meadows, the woods. Even on the slope on the other side of the bridge and in the Moserwald. And if she only went up at irregular intervals it increased the risk that she would be noticed. Recently she had met children playing and women gathering wood. They had watched her!

And Felix, Felix! She was almost surprised that he had never been in the bunker before. Perhaps he was afraid of the silence, the darkness, whatever might be waiting for him in that labyrinth? Or did he trust her so much that he was really not suspicious any more? She couldn't very well ask him. But if he didn't suspect that there was a Russian in the bunker, why did he sometimes look at her so strangely? When she eventually fell asleep, she saw herself hanging – with a placard around her neck, on which was written: I AM A TRAITOR.

Although there was now another woman helping out at the Lamb, she had to be trained first. And in any case, Mother was convinced that Hedi was irreplaceable. That meant that Anna was sometimes allowed to be in charge of the rations in the kitchen on her own.

'Just don't be too generous!' Mother called to her. 'It has to balance with the coupons, or we'll be in a hell of a mess!'

Those damned coupons. Since the beginning of March, there was a lot less – of nearly everything.

Spring always came later in Stiegnitz than in Schonberg, which lay lower down in the valleys. A snowstorm was still raging in the middle of March. But now, on the day before Palm Sunday, it had all thawed out again. Anna picked snowdrops near the barricade at the eastern end of the village. She brought a bunch into the Lamb and put it in a glass on the bar. She gave a second bunch to Grandmother. She put it on the household altar. Anna hid a third in her bedroom.

When she came back into the living room, Grandmother was looking for her glasses.

'I had them a moment ago,' she complained. 'Come and help me look. They can't be far!'

Anna searched with her: on the little altar, on the dresser, on the windowsills. Funny: she had no idea whether Grandmother was shortsighted or longsighted. Probably longsighted. Like most old people. She asked.

'No, not longsighted!' Grandmother cried nervously. 'I've always been extremely shortsighted! And now I've got to go to the Lamb and I can't find my glasses!'

'You can make do with one of your spare pairs for a while,' said Mother, who was already putting her coat on. 'After all, you've got two.'

Grandmother ran to her room and fetched them.

But just as she was about to slip into her own coat, she discovered the missing pair on the edge of the stove. 'Thank God!' she cried, grabbed them and put the spare pair in Anna's hand. 'Will you put them back in my room please,' she asked and left the house with Mother.

167

Anna took the spare glasses – and thought of Maxim. Why not try this pair too?

As she tiptoed out of her room on the morning of Palm Sunday, the rucksack full of leftover food and the pigs' potatoes, Grandmother was already at church. Mother and Felix were still asleep. The whole house smelled of Grandmother's plaited Easter pastries.

Anna was already halfway down the stairs when Donar began to bark. He yapped so loudly that Mother called out sleepily from downstairs to see what was wrong, and Felix came out of his room.

'Nothing!' Anna called loudly. 'It's only me.' And she whispered to her brother: 'You know – I'm going to think of poems.'

'I don't understand you,' Felix said sleepily. 'You've finally got a chance to sleep in. But instead you've got to write poems. As if that was so important. You can understand Grandmother storming off to early Mass. Religion. But you – just for poems?'

Anna relaxed a bit. He still seemed to really believe in the fairy tale of poems! Oh Felix! Did he really have no doubts about what she had served up to him because he trusted her? Or didn't he want to doubt her lies, so as not to have to live with a sister who in his eyes was a traitor?

'And why are you taking the snowdrops with you?' asked Felix in astonishment.

She hadn't been prepared for that. Of course – why was she carrying snowdrops around the countryside if she wanted to write poems? It took a bit too long before something occurred to her: 'I thought I'd give them to the first person I met.'

'That's me!' cried Felix, and stretched out his hand.

'So it is,' she answered and handed him the bunch. 'They're for luck.'

He smiled at her. Now he was her sweet brother again, like he used to be. So attached to her. And so full of desire to be liked. She smiled back.

'I hope you have lots of inspiration,' he whispered back to her, and calling the dog, disappeared back into his room.

Pity – she couldn't take the snowdrops to Maxim now. But it had been worth it to give them to Felix. She had managed to brighten up the mood between them. That was very valuable. She set off feeling confident. It would all turn out well – somehow!

She heard tits twittering and larks warbling.

And the buds were about to burst. Her eye fell on a young birch. If Maxim put the twigs in water, somewhere where they got some light, they would sprout leaves. Not a lot earlier than they would outside. But that wasn't the point. The important thing was that he would at least have something living there with him. Young birch green in the bunker – that was spring too!

She didn't just have food, candles and batteries in the rucksack, but scissors and a mirror. And the glasses.

Maxim was glad about all the things she brought, and especially the birch twigs. Wasn't the birch native to Russia too? He smelled the twigs. But as Anna pulled the glasses out of her coat pocket, he gave her the branch to hold and grasped the glasses with both hands. Carefully he put them on, looked around, looked at Anna – and then he picked her up firmly by the waist, swung her around in a circle and set her back on her feet, before she had even properly grasped what had happened to her.

She had never seen him so glad, so happy. His sight must have been really bad if he was so pleased with Grandmother's glasses. They couldn't be exactly right for his prescription. But he could obviously see a great deal better with them than without.

That morning, Anna cut Maxim's wildly sprouting mane and clipped his beard. Afterwards he didn't need to hold the mirror right up to his face.

It wasn't until she was on her way home that she realised that she hadn't been afraid of him. She shook her head in amusement. Afraid of Maxim? Ridiculous!

As she ran down the slope, she pictured him, wearing the glasses, unfolding the hiking map and looking for a route into the Protectorate. Then a sudden inspiration had come to her, she had made a split-second decision. Could she be responsible for letting him go now? They hadn't been discovered in all this time. Why couldn't that stay the same for the next few weeks, until the war was finally over? Now Maxim didn't need to take the risk of a flight into the Czech area, the search for a new hiding place. No. She had shaken her head and pointed to the flags on her map which showed where the fronts ran. The flags were very close now. And Maxim had nodded thoughtfully.

No, she considered it again, if he set off into the unknown once more – how she would worry about him! It was nearly Easter. What was it that Gisela had said in Schonberg? The war would be over by Easter at the latest.

'The church has never been as full as it was today,' Grandmother told them at lunchtime. 'And there were so many people in black...'

Yes, she looked for her glasses for a while. However they were only one of her spare pairs. They'd turn up again sooner or later. Grandmother had more important things to do at the moment.

She spent the whole of Palm Sunday afternoon painting Easter eggs. Anna and Felix helped her. But Grandmother's eggs were the prettiest. They spent a couple of really cosy hours, while outside it poured with rain.

'It's a pity Seff can't be here too,' said Felix. 'He always painted such funny faces on the eggs.'

'There'll be another letter from him this week,' said Grandmother. 'I can feel it in my bones.'

While they were painting the eggs, pure harmony had ruled between Anna and Felix. In the evening when Grandmother had already gone to bed and Mother wasn't yet back from the Lamb, they huddled together on the sofa in the living room. 'What do you think it'll be like when all this is over?' asked Anna.

Felix's face froze. 'Don't believe that I'm one of those who've already given up,' he said darkly. 'It's true that we're in a very unfavourable situation at the moment. But so was Frederick the Great, when the Russians occupied Berlin. He'd chucked the whole pack out again, before they'd even had time to plunder the place properly. The situation seemed really hopeless for Old Fritz then. And it'll be just like that this time. We're a long way from exhausting our reserves. And there are whole year groups of young people standing ready, who haven't been deployed at all yet!' Anna let him talk. His cheeks were glowing, his eyes sparkling, his gestures were getting grander and grander. The blond curl fell into his face again. He was so carried away that he forgot to push the hair back. No, if she tried now to convince him of the impending, unavoidable end, she would fall out with him irreparably.

'Belief in the *Führer*,' cried Felix, 'doesn't just mean being behind him when it's going well for us. Belief in him means *always* standing by him and being prepared to fight and die for him! Then – after a difficult emergency, through which we have to stand firm now – things will go upwards again, from victory to victory. And one day the whole of Europe will belong to us, to Moscow and beyond. Then the text *From the Maas to Memel, from the Etsch to the Belt* will no longer apply! Shall I show you all that on the map?'

He jumped up eagerly and ran towards the chest of drawers.

'No,' she cried, shocked, 'I can imagine it. Come back to the sofa and don't make such a fuss!'

He turned round disappointedly. 'When the war's over,' he said dreamily, 'the first thing I'll do is go on a tour of the whole of the Great German Empire. The colonies above all.'

'You mean, if you're still alive then,' Anna threw in, without giving her voice an ironic undertone. He looked at her so seriously, that in that moment she was unspeakably sorry for him.

'Yes,' he said. 'I might be killed.'

'And if you were lucky and came out of it with your life – what would you do *after* the tour?'

'I've never thought that far in the future,' said Felix pensively. 'I've only imagined landing on an island at the end of the journey. On an island with palm trees, where the beach is yellow and the water's blue-green. And where those really brightly coloured parrots fly around my ship. And I'd be completely alone on the ship and on the island, and everything, everything, would belong to me.'

'I've dreamt of that sort of thing too,' said Anna. 'I've often thought about what I'd take to an island like that, if it could only be one thing.'

'Do you have to think about that?' asked Felix in amazement. 'I'd know at once what it'd be. The German flag of course! I would fly it in the middle of the island.'

'The only thing I was sure of then,' mused Anna, 'was that it would be a person. But who – that was the problem! Sometimes it was Mother, sometimes Seff, sometimes Grandmother, according to who I particularly liked at the time. Sometimes even you.'

'Me?' wondered Felix, beaming at her.

'Why? Are you surprised?' she asked. 'You *are* my brother, Felix.'

He lowered his gaze. 'If I had to take a person with me, Anna, it wouldn't be you. For me there's only one...'

'Hitler,' said Anna.

He nodded. Then he looked at her and said: 'Anyway, this is all just a game. But you were thinking in the right way. Why on earth have you become so different...?'

'Perhaps it's because I'm a bit older than you. Then you don't just trust everything that the adults tell you any longer. Then you start to think for yourself and to be critical. Then you start to look behind things. For example...'

'No,' he said hastily. 'Be quiet. I don't want to start to doubt. If all that, the Idea I mean, was really just lies and deception, then what would all the many, many soldiers have died for?'

She could only shrug. She made as if to carry on talking, but he shook his head. His face took on a tortured expression. So Anna put her hand on his and said with a smile: 'How about a star at the top of the mast instead of the flag – that wouldn't be bad, would it?'

'I'll stick to the flag,' he answered, his brows drawn together.

'And what about Donar? Would you leave him here?'

'He's in second place. But I wouldn't have to think about him anyway. He'd come swimming after me.'

17

On Maundy Thursday, the postwoman brought the news that Seff had been killed at Breslau.

Grandmother ran into the village crying loudly, to Felix and Mother. They shut the Lamb for three days. Mother went home and lay down on her bed. Nobody was allowed in to her, not even Anna and Felix. She only allowed Grandmother to bring her tea a few times. When Grandmother tried to talk to her, she sent her away.

The three of them sat distraught together in the living room, Grandmother, Anna and Felix, until the visitors came to express their condolence. Mother didn't let anyone talk to her. So it was Grandmother who accepted all the condolences. On Good Friday, Uncle Franz stood with her too.

Many, many people came, including relatives from the neighbouring villages, and Grandmother had her hands full: a little drink of schnapps or a coffee and a grateful handshake for everyone. And she had also thought to put a black ribbon around Seff's photo.

On that day, Anna saw Uncle Franz cry for the first time. He, having no children of his own, had been as fond of Seff as if he had been his own son. And Aunt Agnes sobbed: 'But he was to have been our heir!'

Felix skulked around in corners, his face disturbed, when he wasn't behind the shed practising shooting. For hours. When Grandmother wanted to fetch him into the house because more visitors had arrived, he fought her off gruffly.

'Leave me alone! I'm going to avenge him.'

There was still no end to the visits on Holy Saturday. Some people sat there for hours, let themselves be helped to Easter pastries, and moved on from Seff's death to talk about the general situation. Gloomily, they related that Danzig had fallen and Frankfurt had been occupied by the Americans. They sighed and asked Grandmother whether she had buried her silver spoons yet. She jumped in shock and said: 'But they won't come here.'

The guests shook their heads. You could never know. After all, you'd never have thought that Danzig —

'But that's a lot further away!' cried Grandmother.

'And Frankfurt . . .'

Grandmother just dismissed the idea. Not here. Never here!

Friday night was the second night when Anna didn't sleep a wink. Seff dead. Unimaginable. Was he lying somewhere on a beach? Had his comrades had enough time to bury him?

'Father,' she said quietly to the photo, 'Seff is dead.'

She shut her eyes and hoped to fall asleep and then to wake up in the happy knowledge that it had all just been a bad dream.

But she didn't fall asleep.

On Saturday evening, she could no longer stand the

176

constant 'my deepest sympathy!' She went out into the darkness, let herself go where chance took her. She had the torch with her, as always.

Lost in thought she wandered off. Seff. Oh, Seff. He had fallen at Breslau. So he had been killed by Russians. And she was hiding and caring for a Russian soldier!

Without having consciously chosen her route, she was suddenly standing in front of the bunker. She took a deep breath. Now that she was here she went in, full of desperation, rage and grief. Seff would never come back. Never, never! And all the fuss with their damned sympathy. And Maxim, who couldn't help it, but was still a Russian. And all the madness ruling around her! She beat her fists against the concrete wall of the corridor. That did some good.

Tap-tap, tap-tap. He was waiting for her by the doorway and greeted her quietly, in what seemed to her to be a nervous mood. The glasses reflected the light from her torch.

She had arrived unannounced and later than ever before. Enough reason for his '*Dobro pozhalovat*' to sound uneasy.

'Seff is dead!' she said. And then she dug her fingers into his coat, pulled on it and screamed: 'Seff is dead! Seff!'

He didn't seem to understand. He freed her hands from his clothes with a firm grip and pushed Anna ahead of him into the side corridor. When she didn't stop screaming, he pressed his hand to her mouth.

So he pushed her as far as his rooms, his camp,

pushed her down, barked at her. She let herself fall onto the sleeping bag, turned over and leant against the cold wall. Covering her face with her hands, she began to cry.

Maxim crouched in front of her and whispered worriedly: 'Yeva...Yeva!'

She carried on sobbing unrestrainedly. He took her by the shoulders and shook her. 'Yeva!'

She couldn't stop. For two whole days she had held it all in, controlled herself. Now it all burst out of her. Seff! Seff!

Through her tears, she saw Maxim's shocked eyes quite close to her, behind his glasses, and his scar. She realised that he had gone away, heard his steps coming closer again. She jumped as she felt something cold touching her fingers. He held out a cup of water to her and she drank hastily.

How big – and how empty – the room was. Nothing but the candles on the floor. When Maxim walked over behind the flames, his gigantic ghostly shadow flickered on the walls and the blanket.

He took the empty cup from her again and passed her the packet of chalk. Of course, he didn't even know why she was crying. Kneeling, she drew her family on the wall again, crossed Seff out and drew a cross next to him. Then she dropped the chalk and burst into tears again. But now she pressed her own hands to her mouth.

Maxim sat down next to her and put his arm around her. He spoke to her quietly. She didn't understand what he was saying, but his gentle, quiet murmuring calmed her, released her, made her sleepy. All at once, she suddenly felt very, very tired. Her eyes fell shut. If only she could sleep, sleep!

She let herself fall to her side and curled up. Already half-asleep, she felt him taking the rucksack off her, pulling the sleeping bag under her, covering her.

Anna slept until the early morning. A light woke her, moving in front of her closed eyelids. She opened her eyes and saw that Maxim was crouching in front of the camp circling a candle in front of her. He was whispering something and making signals: Get up, get up! Then he put the candle down, stood up and beat his arms. He was freezing! He hopped, did knee-bends, press-ups, beat his arms again.

'Maxim!' She jumped up and passed him the sleeping bag. He wrapped it around himself and made signs to her to follow him. In the room which was half under water, she washed her face under the rivulet that dripped down from the ceiling. Maxim held out his towel to her. It stank. She laid her hand on his arm and said: 'I'm sorry.'

Had he understood what she wanted to say to him? He nodded and stroked her hair. She felt her eyes filling with tears again. Oh, Seff!

He gave her another drink. The water was icy cold. He filled the cup again from the rivulet and drank now himself.

'Happy Easter,' she whispered, while the tears ran over her cheeks again. It hurt so much to think about Seff.

As she set off again and crossed the room in which she had slept, there was no longer a candle burning there. She let the beam of her torch run over the walls. Hadn't she drawn something there? But there was nothing left. Only a cross.

At home nobody had missed her. Anna heard Grandmother rumbling around in her room, heard that Mother was washing. And upstairs Donar was yapping. She went into the living room and sat down at the table. After a while, Mother appeared, all in black, and sat down opposite her. They sat there in silence. It was completely quiet. Only the clock was ticking.

Anna realised that today was the first of April. April Fool's Day: You've got a hole in your stocking! Or: Your bun's come undone! Or: Run to the shops, they've got chocolate without coupons!

What if Seff were to come through the door now and laugh, 'April Fool!'...

Grandmother appeared in the living room.

'We must go and see the priest about the funeral Mass,' she said.

'You do it,' answered Mother. 'I'm dealing with the notice in the paper.'

'What will happen to his things?' asked Anna.

'They stay right where they are,' answered Mother sharply. 'All of them!'

They went to the Easter Mass together, all in black.

Even Felix. He was wearing Seff's Sunday suit. He didn't own anything else that was dark enough apart from his First Communion suit, and he'd grown out of that long ago.

Donar howled after Felix. But Mother stood firm. The dog was not coming into the church!

The priest preached about the Resurrection. Anna saw Grandmother and Aunt Agnes crying. She thought of Seff's corduroy trousers and his loden jacket which Maxim had worn. Would Seff have minded that his things had been borrowed by a Russian? But he was in danger of his life, Seff, you understand that, don't you!

With half an ear she heard Grandmother whisper: 'Well he's got the Resurrection over with now.'

The house would probably be full of visitors today too. Oh the poor boy, still so young. But he's got this vale of tears behind him now, who knows what's still to come. Oh poor you, poor us. They say the Russians are like animals, they don't leave a single woman alone, and even those who are still little more than children – and they've already reached Danzig...

No, not another day like that. She would travel to Gisela in Schonberg. Today.

Despite Grandmother's protests she set off after the meal on the path to Mellersdorf, with the shopping bag and rucksack.

'Let her go,' Mother had said. 'It'll give her something else to think about.'

But when she reached Mellersdorf station, she learned that she couldn't get a ticket without official confirmation of the necessity of her visit to Schonberg. And her school season ticket had expired.

181

Defeated, she turned back. So she wouldn't see Gisela again until the war was over. And after that? Only if they were both still alive. Anna remembered her exact words: 'All that matters now is whether we survive the End, into the peace. No easy task, I'm afraid . . .'

On the Tuesday after Easter some post arrived: a letter and a card. The card showed a huge bunch of daffodils with Easter greetings underneath. To Anna with all good wishes from Gisela.

The letter was from Seff. He was well, it wasn't so cold any more, and he had seen snowdrops already. Happy Easter! – in case he didn't get another chance to write before the festival.

The letter had taken over three weeks to arrive. Seff, poor Seff.

18

Mother was back in the Lamb, albeit in black. Life went on. And how it went on! They said that on a still day you could already hear the thunder of artillery, over on the eastern slopes of the Eberberg.

Anna went for a walk on the Eberberg on a still morning and there was a rumbling in the distance. Three days later she even heard it as she went up the slope to the bunker, and that was west-facing.

Maxim seemed restless as he greeted her. He led her into one of the dark rooms near his room with the hole in the roof and turned the torch on something lying on the floor. It was a large sheepdog. Dead. Bloodstains stood out on the floor.

Maxim had beaten it to death. He pointed to an iron pipe leaning in a corner. It was the same pipe that Anna had used at first to mark the entrance hole in the main corridor. He must have kept hold of it in case he needed it. She remembered having seen it next to his camp on her last few visits.

She could imagine the dog rushing in here barking, baring its teeth at Maxim, perhaps even leaping at him. And the noise! What else could Maxim have done but kill it?

There was no doubt: the dog had followed her trail from Holy Saturday. And Maxim would have had to assume that there were men following the dog, searching for him.

But nobody had come.

Now they carried the dead animal together through the main corridor deeper into the mountain – to a chamber that lay far off to the side.

It made Anna think about Felix. What if it had been Donar! How Felix would search for the dog, how he would mourn him!

But Maxim was alive and unharmed.

At home Grandmother was saying that people already seemed to have begun eating dogs.

The Grubners' beautiful sheepdog had vanished without a trace a few days ago. It had been faithfulness itself. It had prowled around a lot, but it had always come home in the evenings.

Felix, now constantly in uniform, having finally received the *Führer*'s stripe he had been desperately longing for – five days after Easter – had only one topic of conversation: the defence of the village.

'If they should really overcome our barricades,' he shouted, 'which is practically impossible, then there'll be a house to house battle! Our farm is in a particularly strategically advantageous position!'

'There'll be no shooting here,' answered Mother determinedly. 'And Stiegnitz will surrender without a fight. Do you think I'm going to watch them shoot my second son down too? And do you think I'm going to let them shoot the Lamb to pieces around me? We make our living from the inn regardless of who is in charge of the country. I'm warning you. If you pick up your pop-gun on the day they arrive, I'll give you such a clout that you'll miss your shot, you snotty-nosed brat!' She was in such a rage that Felix didn't dare contradict her. But Anna could see nothing but defiance in his face.

Once Anna surprised Mother and Grandmother behind the barn on the edge of the forest. They were digging a hole. A couple of Uncle Franz's tins and a little chest stood beside them, tightly sealed.

'What are you doing?' asked Anna in surprise.

Mother jumped and Grandmother shrieked, 'Mother of God!'

'Oh! You made me jump!' said Mother, and Grandmother explained: 'It's only the most valuable things. Just to be on the safe side. You can never know. Until things are calmer again.'

So it had got that far. And it was unrolling ever faster. The Americans had already reached Thuringia, Königsberg had already surrendered. The war was creeping closer and closer. There was a notice on the blackboard which stated clearly that hanging out white flags, opening barricades that had been closed or trying to escape without an express order to evacuate would be strictly punished. All male inhabitants of any house where a white flag appeared were to be shot.

Once Anna heard Felix shouting at Grandmother,

inflamed with rage: 'You're acting just as if he wasn't there any more!' And he added: 'He'll have his reasons for waiting so long with the counterattack!'

Anna knew who he was talking about.

She dreamed about Seff. She saw him sitting in the Lamb with Maxim. They were playing cards together. Hedi was serving. Seff roared with laughter, just as he had always done, Maxim was laughing too, out loud without pressing his hand to his mouth.

One morning Anna was woken by a loud knocking on the front door. Donar began to yap. Anna looked at her watch. Just before five. Nobody in the house was up yet. She always got up just before six to listen to the radio. Who wanted anything so early?

She heard Grandmother coming out of her room and shuffling to the front door, heard men's voices. Felix was already running down the stairs with Donar. Mother's voice was mixed in among the noise too.

As Anna came into the living room, still half asleep, there were two German soldiers sitting there in front of the stove, obviously unarmed, warming themselves, drinking coffee and cutting themselves thick slices of Grandmother's bread. They seemed to be very hungry. Felix was watching them, holding Donar in his arms. The men were talking to Mother. The war was nearly over now, thank God, and everyone was looking forward to seeing his family again soon.

'Where is your unit stationed?' asked Felix.

One of the troopers glanced at him furtively and then gestured towards the east.

'We're looking for quarters for our people,' said the other, deliberately casually.

'Then you must speak to the mayor of the village,' said Mother.

'Now, don't be hasty,' said the other.

Grandmother whispered to Anna that she should fetch another *Blutwurst* from the cellar. As she appeared with the sausage, she heard her ringing voice: 'That's the way! Nice and fresh! A good breakfast is the most important meal of the day.'

Anna was annoyed. All the things the men were eating were only available on coupons. They couldn't know that the *Blutwurst* didn't come from the butcher's. They were devouring the food as if it was the most natural thing in the world! They didn't even think it was necessary to say thank you.

Only after a while did Anna notice that Felix wasn't there any more. And Donar was howling out in the laundry. Had Felix crawled back to bed? But then why was Donar shut up in the laundry?

When Mother asked the men what they intended to do now, the men only gave a vague answer. They weren't just charged with finding accommodation but also with secretly observing the village. But that had to stay secret, didn't it? Nobody must find out that they were here. Grandmother nodded subserviently, but Mother raised an eyebrow.

'And who will look after you?' she asked.

Well, of course she must take charge of that. After all, they must all pull together, mustn't they?

'Where's the boy gone?' one of them asked suddenly.

Mother looked up, looked around. 'He must have gone back upstairs,' she said. 'After all, it's still the middle of the night.'

The man jumped up and shouted nervously: 'Go and look at once!'

Now Mother had reached the point where she had cast aside her politeness. Anna knew the signs. 'What are you thinking of?' she cried. 'Whether my son is in bed or wandering around outside is nothing to do with you!'

Now the second soldier jumped up too.

'What's wrong, what's wrong?' whimpered Grandmother. 'Keep eating, it's getting cold! The boy hasn't done anything, he's only a child.'

Anna was trying desperately to understand what was going on. While the men rushed to the window which looked out over the yard, she ran up the stairs, pulled open the door to the boys' room and glanced in. Felix wasn't there.

A dreadful suspicion came over her. What if these two soldiers were absent from the troop without leave and were trying to go to ground here – and Felix had run into the village to betray them?

She'd have to warn them, shout to them: 'Run for the forest! Run for your lives!'

The noise downstairs got louder. Men's voices roared, doors slammed. Anna rushed down.

It was already too late. The village policeman was just

coming through the front door, Felix behind him, beaming, with a gun in his hand. Donar was yapping like mad in the laundry.

The two privates had no chance. With the rifle at the ready, the policeman made them walk in front of him, down the slope to the bridge, into the village. Felix went with him.

'I don't understand anything any more,' said Grand-mother in surprise. 'They were on our side!'

Anna was bursting with anger. Granted, the two of them had been unpleasant. But just to betray them? They would shoot them or hang them, probably even today, with cardboard placards around their necks: I AM A DESERTER.

'Why didn't you warn them?' she shouted at Mother.

'Warn them? Why?' wailed Grandmother. 'Tell me what's going on...'

'I'd only just realised what they were myself,' sighed Mother letting herself slump into a chair. 'But even if I'd got it straight away, I don't think I'd have dared to warn them. Felix is capable of denouncing me.'

Grandmother was now gradually grasping what it was about. She crossed herself and began to cry: 'What kind of godless world is this, when parents are afraid of their children!'

Anna couldn't believe it. Mother was afraid of Felix, a fourteen-year-old boy. Mother, who had always been so courageous!

Felix came back swelling with pride. 'What do you say now?' he cried. 'I was the only one who noticed and acted on it. You're all so unsuspecting, so innocent! And you could practically smell that they were deserters!'

'Did that *have* to happen?' yammered Grandmother. 'Why did they have to come to us? Nothing but trouble! And then – if they survive, they might come back after the war to get revenge!'

Typical Grandmother. She didn't feel bound to act decently to strangers.

'Don't worry,' said Felix dismissively, 'they won't survive. Probably not even until this evening. They make short work of traitors.'

Anna stared at him. She shuddered. He thought he had done a good deed! Now she no longer doubted that he would denounce her, his sister, if he found her out.

The next time Anna left the house to go to the bunker, Donar came running after her. She tried in vain to shoo him back.

'Take him with you!' Felix called after her. 'He won't disturb your you-know-what. He'll just curl up and doze.'

'But I don't want to have him there!' she shouted furiously.

Felix whistled the dog back with a searching look. She watched Donar until he disappeared into the house. Although he was nearly full-grown – he must be about four months now – he was still clumsy and playful. Just right for cuddling and stroking. But not in the bunker! And if Donar learned the way to Maxim, he'd be sure to lead Felix there too.

When she looked round again, she noticed Felix at the

window of his room. So he was watching her. As carelessly as possible she waved to him.

The grass was green again, the first anemones and cowslips were blooming, the path was muddy. All the paths squelched, oozed, splashed underfoot. The forest swayed in a gentle breeze, white clouds ran across the sky. Just a few more days and there would be leaves on the trees again, it would sparkle in a thousand shades of green!

Maxim had got rid of all the blood stains from the dead dog on the concrete floor. Anna saw that he had scrubbed it with roots and clumps of grass. His knuckles were rubbed raw.

This time he hardly hid his interest in the flags.

One beyond Vienna, one before Berlin, a whole row along the southern border of Silesia – dangerously close. He bent over the map. Then he turned to her and spoke. It seemed that he had a request. But she didn't understand him. Then he took a piece of chalk and drew a uniform – *his* uniform! Anna nodded. He needed it now. But would it still be usable after so long under the stones and moss? And if so, how could she wash it without being seen? That would only be possible up here.

A letter arrived from Schonberg. It contained the order to report to the Girls' Section Leader's department on Wednesday 18th April 1945, at ten thirty am, to answer for frequent absence without leave from League Sport Duty.

Anna glanced at the calendar. The 18th April was tomorrow. She was about to crumple up the letter and throw it in the stove when it occurred to her that it might carry enough weight to convince the railway official in Mellersdorf to sell her a ticket.

She let Mother know what she was doing, left Grandmother to her laments and ran to Mellersdorf at a jog. Gisela – I'm coming!

But the man behind the counter just shook his head.

'To Schonberg? Are you mad? They're evacuating the town now...'

19

Mother decided not to take any more guests in the Lamb until it was all over. But that didn't mean that she was cooking any less. Hordes of refugees came through the village – in lorries, in cars, on foot. They had to be fed. Red Cross nurses appeared, helped out. Anna kept an eye out for Gisela, asked after people from Schonberg. But it seemed that they were being taken somewhere else. After all, you weren't allowed to decide for yourself where you would be evacuated to. While Anna helped to look after the children and old people and lent Mother a hand in the kitchen, she learned that two soldiers had been hanged for desertion in the city. And that the mayor of one of the neighbouring villages had shot himself.

Now she could even hear the dull rumbling of the artillery from her bedroom window if she opened it for a while in the mornings. It sounded eerie. Ominous. Schonberg evacuated. Only about fifty kilometres away, less as the crow flies. Gisela's house empty, the school, the Café Paris – all empty. Perhaps even destroyed. Mother didn't even come home at night any more. She was smothering her grief with work.

The lovage shrubs in Grandmother's garden were putting out new leaves, the chives were sprouting, the lilac buds were swelling and the whole slope of the meadow in front of the house was studded with cowslips.

On a warm afternoon, when the sun kept breaking through, Anna dared to dig Maxim's uniform out of the pile of stones. It wasn't yet disintegrating under her fingers; it hadn't yet been gnawed by mice. She put the bucket with the potatoes for the pigs in the rucksack, placed a quarter of a loaf on top with a few leftovers from the Lamb. There weren't very many of them now, it had become a matter of every last crumb. She spread the uniform over the bucket. How full the rucksack was!

And a piece of laundry soap as well. And the exercise book together with a pen in an outside pocket. Just in case.

'I'm going to pick cowslips!' she called to Grand-mother, who was in the garden behind the shed digging over a flowerbed.

Just as she reached the bridge, she met Felix. He was in a hurry. Donar was romping around him. His lead was dragging along the ground.

'We've got *Volkssturm* roll-call in a minute,' panted Felix. 'It was announced at very short notice. We're getting guns and ammunition. I can't take Donar with me. Will you take him home?'

She took the dog in her arms and wrapped the lead around her hand. Donar stretched over her shoulder and began to snuffle at the rucksack. She tried to pull his head round to the front, but he carried on snuffling stubbornly.

'What have you got in there?' asked Felix in surprise.

194

Anna felt her pulse racing. 'My boots,' she said, 'as usual. And something to eat. And a blanket.'

He grabbed the rucksack and felt it. 'Feels like a bucket,' he said.

'For the boots,' she answered, as the world began to spin around her. 'Otherwise they make the rucksack and the blanket muddy.'

'Strange,' he said, 'that you can still think about things like that. When Seff—'

'That's the whole point!' she shouted. 'You always write poems about the thing that's going round your head the most. They're about Seff, believe me!'

'Believe you . . . ' he repeated slowly. He glanced at his watch. 'Oh well, see you later,' he said and turned to go.

She breathed out. That had gone well again. It didn't bear thinking about what would have happened if he had tussled with her for the rucksack, won it and unpacked it!

But now he turned round, came back. She held her breath.

'What is it?' she asked lightly.

He looked at her. She avoided his eyes and played about with Donar.

'Anna,' he said, 'look at me.'

She raised her head. Their eyes met.

'What is it then?' she asked roughly. 'I thought you were in a hurry? If you aren't, then you can take your god of thunder home on your own.'

Felix seemed not to hear what she said. He looked at her fixedly and asked: '*Have* you hidden someone?'

'Rubbish,' she answered violently. 'You're obsessed.

I showed you where I go. Now shut up about it. Your constant suspicion is really making me ill!'

Once again, Felix seemed not to hear her. He came so close to her that she had to take a step backwards.

'What's the matter with you?' she asked indignantly.

'Anna, give me your word of honour,' he said, emphasising every word, 'your word of honour, that you haven't hidden anyone.'

Her word of honour! She was shocked. Until now, she and her brothers, Seff too, had always been able to rely on the word of honour among themselves. It was an unwritten law. She had *never* lied on her word of honour before!

'That's silly,' she said. 'Making all this fuss because of your crazy suspicions.'

'Answer my question!'

'Don't be so childish!'

'You're evading the question!' He wouldn't be shaken off.

'Yes!' she shouted at him. 'If you absolutely have to hear it. I haven't hidden anyone! On my word of honour!'

His face relaxed. He sighed with relief. 'Thank God,' he said and ran off.

Don't think about it, don't think about it yet! She ran back to the farm and took Donar to Grandmother.

'Tie him to the garden fence,' said Grandmother. 'I'll take him into the house in a while.'

She tied the lead up tightly and ran away, followed by Donar's yowling. She had to get away before Grandmother started asking questions!

As she walked up the slope to the bunker, she felt sick. She had lied on her word of honour, had abused the ritual that had been almost sacred to her. Was she dishonourable now?

But should she have delivered Maxim – and herself – up to her brother just for the sake of the damned word of honour?

The miserable feeling, the bad conscience, must be the price she had to pay for taking her head out of the noose.

Anna had almost reached the bunker when Donar came panting up. He was dragging the lead behind him. He had obviously got away from Grandmother. Now what?

Joyfully he jumped up at her, making an infernal racket.

No, she couldn't possibly take him into the bunker. He would immediately search for the other dog, bark and find Maxim. There might be someone nearby to hear the yapping and start paying attention!

She considered desperately. Should she tie the dog up somewhere until she came out of the bunker again? But then he'd howl and whimper so loudly that they'd hear him down in the village. Perhaps children would run to see what it was – or Felix!

Go back again? No. The uniform would need a few days to dry. And as things stood, Maxim would need to wear it very soon.

She picked up Donar's lead and tried to send him home. That was hopeless. He had no intention of pushing off; rather he jumped up and circled round her excitedly.

Then she got angry. The damned dog. She picked up a pebble and threw it at him, but missed. Donar pounced on the stone, his tail wagging, took it in his mouth and brought it back.

Then she just saw red. She picked up a big lump of stone and hurled it at the animal. This time she hit him. Donar crawled a few paces toward her, and then he lay still, without moving.

Silence. Anna drew back, horrified. She hadn't meant to do that – not that! She picked up the stone. It was dripping with blood. She threw it as far as she could into the bushes and ran into the bunker. Get away, get away!

She unpacked the potatoes, bread, leftover noodles and soap in front of Maxim. And the uniform. Visibly moved, he spread it out. She helped him to fill the buckets. The water in the flooded room was now more than a hand span deep. They scooped it up with the pot and cup. Then Maxim shaved soap flakes into the water and soaked his uniform, the coat in Anna's bucket, tunic and trousers in Gisela's.

He wouldn't let her help with the washing. He pointed to the map. She should move the flags! She stuck them round Berlin, on the Elbe near Torgau, in Brünn. Then she leant against the wall and watched him.

Maxim was kneeling by the two buckets, soaping and scrubbing in one, rinsing in the other, a couple of times he tipped out the dirty water. Now and then he threw Anna an encouraging glance. But she stayed serious. Let him think what he liked. She had many reasons to be serious.

Oh, if only Donar would turn up suddenly! He could yap, whine and whimper, however dangerous it was for her. Somehow everything would carry on working out, after it had gone so well for so long. How could she meet Felix now?

Anna waited until Maxim no longer needed the bucket. Then she left. Let him rack his brains about where to hang the things to dry on his own. Perhaps Donar was only unconscious? Perhaps he was slightly injured – had run home on his own a long time ago? For once she was in a hurry to leave the bunker.

But Donar was still lying there and was already cold. She picked him up and carried him home.

Felix was waiting for her outside the house with eyes red from crying. Why? Had he realised what had happened? As he recognised what she was carrying, he stormed towards her, pulled the dead animal from her arms, pressed it to himself, stroked it tenderly and secretly wiped away the tears that were running down his cheeks.

She was so sorry for him. She wanted to put her arms around him, but he jumped when she touched him. He pulled away from her and stared at her wildly.

'It's my fault,' she said, and now she was crying too. 'I got so angry when he wouldn't go away. So I threw a stone at him. That's what happened. I'm sorry, Felix, I'm so sorry!'

'Murderer!' he shouted.

What could she say to that? Her head bowed, she went behind him into the house. Something like that would never have happened to Seff. He didn't have fits of rage.

It wasn't until they reached the living room that she learned why Felix had been crying when he waited for her: Hitler was dead.

Her first thought was: Now it'll soon be over. She would only have to hold on for a few more days, perhaps not even another week!

And Felix? Everything must have collapsed around him, his whole world until now. And Donar's death on top of that. She decided to be particularly caring with her brother in the next few days, as if he was a convalescing invalid.

Hitler dead. Even six months ago she might have felt like weeping at the news.

Felix buried Donar under the lilac. He didn't talk to Anna for the next few days. He didn't even look at her. He even avoided spending time in the house, as far as possible. When he wasn't helping in the Lamb, he stood near the entrance to the village, by the side of the road, and watched the columns of German troops who passed through the village.

Wenzel Krause stood there too. For hours. And when a lorry trundled past, full of escaping soldiers, or a car of Party bigwigs in mufti rolled by, hooting at him impatiently, he raised his arm in a stiff salute and crowed, '*Heil Hitler!*' with all his heart.

Until his mother found him and dragged him away.

20

Now even Grandmother believed it. The Russians were coming, as surely as night follows day. And soon at that. Very soon. In a few days. Holy Mary Mother of God! She set half an hour aside and prayed fervently in front of her little household altar. She ordered Anna to pray too, but she just shook her head and took herself out of the living room.

'Seff just had to get through these few weeks more, then he would have stayed alive!' Grandmother complained. 'Why didn't you hold your hand over him, Lord God?'

She moaned like that a lot now.

'There is no God,' said Felix darkly.

'Jesus and Mary,' she exclaimed, 'where have you picked *that* up from? How are you going to get through times like these without the Lord God!'

In the next few days, hordes of German soldiers surged westwards over the mountains together with columns of refugees. Anna too sometimes stood at the roadside watching them.

Only a few privates took the time to swallow a hasty bowl of soup in the Lamb. Just get away from the danger of ending up a prisoner of the Russians!

The flight of the soldiers became more hectic every day. They threw their weapons, their packs, into the ditches, left their guns, their cars behind, as soon as the tanks were empty, they threw away anything that was a hindrance to their flight. Military files fluttered through the village, untended horses grazed on the dandelion yellow meadows. The fleeing troops tried to get to safety across country.

When there were no more troops flooding in from the East, the villagers gathered up the food that lay scattered across the fields, wet with spring rain: sacks of sugar and rice, cartons of margarine, milk powder, sides of bacon, canisters of oil, even hundreds of bars of chocolate from a supply depot. There were things that they had never set eyes on before: brown sugar, ground coconut, Dutch cheeses, Crimean Sekt and Russian caviar.

Felix and Anna swarmed out too and brought home as much as they could carry. Mother now had more than enough ingredients for the inn kitchen. But there were no longer any guests, since the last soldiers, the last refugees, had disappeared over the mountains. The women from Castrop-Rauxel who were living in the Lamb helped her to hide the valuable things they found behind the sheets of ice – for when it was over.

The Czechs who lived in Stiegnitz were collecting things too. Anna noticed that the German villagers no longer dared to argue with them over particularly good finds. They tried only to cheat each other when fetching the booty.

Mother's thoughts seemed to rush a long way ahead. On one hasty lunchtime she said: 'The Czech flag will soon hang outside the parish office.'

Anna stared at her, shocked. She hadn't dared to

imagine so far into the future! All the same, it was perhaps less than a week until it would happen. The Czechs must already be crouched in the starting blocks, ready to take back the Sudetenland. And now, these very days, they were quite certainly celebrating their liberation. You didn't need a particularly vivid imagination to realise that.

'Now they'll take it out on us Germans,' said Mother darkly. She said it when Felix wasn't there.

Grandmother was amazed by the things her grandchildren were dragging in. Perhaps things wouldn't turn out as badly as they had feared. She stashed the treasures in the cellar and on the barn floor.

Anna had secretly set aside the things she wanted to take to Maxim. At last he would really be able to eat his fill for once!

The village was now in an absolute whirl of rumours. All order had broken down in the surrounding area, there were no longer any authorities, no officials. The District Party Leader was said to have fled in his official car, in mufti, and the Local Group Leader likewise to have made off, with his whole family. The Russians were supposed to be in Glatz already and approaching from the East and South as well. The city was burning – you could see the smoke from the slopes of the Eberberg. They said that there would be a ceasefire after midnight.

So the war was over? Wasn't that a reason for jubilation, for celebration? But Stiegnitz was ruled by naked fear. The Russians, the Russians – would they wreak havoc here? Girls and young women were heading for the forests, they said, you shouldn't wait too long, they could arrive any minute, better to disappear too early than too late. The French were departing laughing and noisy. And there was already a white sheet hanging out of the Lamb.

Anna met Uncle Franz. He looked exhausted. His hair, damp with sweat, hung down in his face. Anna suspected that it wasn't just sweat from working.

'Are you still there?' he asked. 'They'll come soon.'

Felix came running up. 'When do you want the barricades to be closed, Uncle Franz?' he asked.

'Not at all,' answered Uncle Franz quietly. 'The most we'll gain from closed barricades is that they'll reduce our village to rubble.'

'What on earth did we build them all for then?' cried Felix, outraged.

'Because we let ourselves be led by a madman,' said Uncle Franz darkly.

Felix stared at him dumbfounded. 'But think of your speeches! You were for him too!' he shouted.

'I was,' growled Uncle Franz. 'Unfortunately. We all were. Now we'll have to pay dearly for it.'

Felix's voice cracked. 'Now he's dead,' he sobbed, 'you're all abandoning him. Well not me, not me!'

'Have you given back the rifle?' asked Uncle Franz abruptly.

'That doesn't belong to you!' Felix screamed at him. 'That belongs to the *Führer*! And the war will continue – without you lot. You're all faithless! Faithless! And bloody liars!'

Uncle Franz grabbed him by the shoulder but Felix escaped his grip and ran off.

Anna watched after him sadly.

'Look out for the boy,' said Uncle Franz to her. 'He could do something awful. He could bring disaster on our village if he's not stopped. Above all, take the rifle away from him. He's just a child.'

'Now you wonder,' a woman called out to him, as she rushed over, 'why our children don't behave like children any more. When you used them like adults!'

Uncle Franz didn't have an answer for her. 'All of you, hang out white flags,' he said to Anna. 'Spread the word. And see that you make for the forest soon.'

When Anna arrived home, Felix was leaning against the wall. She went up to him. He looked up.

'Go to the bunker,' he said tonelessly. 'Where you always write your poems. They won't look in the bunkers. When it's all clear, I'll let you know.'

It was the first time that he had spoken to her again.

'Please, Felix, give up the rifle,' she said quietly.

His face became defiant. He folded his arms and spat. 'I haven't got it now,' he growled. 'I threw it in the stream.'

He avoided her eyes,

Thrown in the stream. That was a good place for it. She breathed out. So he'd come to his senses.

Slowly he walked over to the lilac bush by the garden fence. He stood there with his head bowed. Probably he now thought Donar was the only faithful person in the world. She went after him and put her arm around him. He leant against her, silently.

'I'll make sure you get another dog,' she whispered. 'A hound. You can call him Donar too…'

Suddenly he turned round and faced her.

'Anna,' he said, 'I *won't* give myself up. I don't want to be one of those who accept the defeat.'

'But what will you do?' she asked in astonishment. 'It's a fact that we've lost the war.'

'It looks like that at the moment,' he answered. 'But that's only a passing phase. Those who are faithful to the *Führer* will regroup, break out of the underground, and then we'll win, win, win!'

He yelled right down her ear so it hurt.

'But Felix,' she said.

He wouldn't be interrupted. 'Listen,' he whispered, 'I've just had a marvellous idea. If they really conquer and occupy the village, we'll go underground in the Moserwald Bunker!'

'Who's we?' asked Anna.

'I'm not alone, you know,' he whispered. 'There are at least four others here in Stiegnitz who'll join in. Two Hitler Youth *Führers* and two *Pimpfe*. And I thought that you could take us supplies there, Anna.'

'Me?' cried Anna, shocked. She thought desperately. 'I'm not brave enough for that. Anyone they caught would be done for!'

No, not again! And anyway, this plan was insane, the purest nonsense! But she couldn't tell him that so drastically. So, how to react?

'I always thought of you as brave,' she heard Felix saying. 'And if they suspected you, you could come out with the stuff about the poems.'

Anna couldn't think clearly. It was enough to make you laugh, all this, laugh and cry!

'You wouldn't last very long in there,' she tried to convince him. 'It's so dark. And you'd be extremely bored. And your families would look for you!'

'Let us worry about that,' he said shortly. 'Our only problem is that we need provisions. Now answer me once and for all: will you help us?'

Anna had to struggle not to laugh. But sadness welled up in her at the same time. She looked at him; saw him hanging on her words, waiting for her answer.

What he was proposing was so pointless. And dangerous at the same time. And all that for an idea which wasn't worth the death of even a single person. An idea that was now only flickering in indoctrinated children like Felix, children who couldn't take it in that their highest ideal was no longer worth anything.

But to deny him this request was impossible now, after all the things he had been through in the last few days. She would have to play along, at least for a while.

'Yes,' she said.

She saw how glad he was. 'I knew it,' he said. 'When it comes to the crunch, we can depend on you!'

Grandmother came racing out of the house and pulled Anna into the living room with her. 'You've got to go,' she said, and pointed to a packet of provisions that she had prepared. There was a thermos flask of coffee there too. And she had got the two horse blankets out ready, along with a towel and soap.

Anna packed it all in her rucksack and secretly added all the things that she had gathered for Maxim from the meadows. She strapped the two blankets over the top.

'The best way to go is directly into the forest behind here,' said Grandmother. 'In the plantation area before the valley. There are others there already.'

'I'm going to the Moserwald Bunker,' answered Anna.

'Will you be alone there?' asked Grandmother with fearful eyes.

Anna said she wouldn't. It was the simple truth.

She put on her best dress, her dancing class dress, and her coat over the top. Hurriedly she grabbed a few more photos from her cupboard and fetched Seff's shaving things out of the boys' room.

'Love to Mother,' she said, saying goodbye to Grandmother.

'I'll pray for you!' she called after her. There she stood in front of the house, in her pinafore and slippers, her hands on top of each other, against her body. That was how she always stood, saying goodbye to someone. Good old Grandmother.

Felix was now standing next to her too and waving. Anna waved back and gazed lovingly over the house, the farmstead on the hill. Her great-grandfather had come into the world here. He had acquired the inn, the Lamb, his son the farm which Uncle Franz worked today. But this little farm on the edge of the forest had always been the focal point of the family. This was her home.

She looked over to the village. There were white flags hanging out everywhere there now: sheets and table-cloths. Only her own house had nothing hanging out yet.

'Hang a sheet from the window!' she cried to Grand-mother and Felix, as loudly as she could.

She saw Felix turn round and disappear into the house.

21

It was a wonderful spring day. The landscape shone dandelion yellow, the birches already shimmered green, larks trilled over the fields. Anna felt so light, so happy. Finally, finally she would be free of the miserable fear, she would no longer be forced to lie and to steal. Maxim was still alive, and the danger was past for him too. She was now no longer responsible for the life of her Russian. Maxim was free, could now help himself to carry on and would be able to embrace his comrades and move on with them, that very day.

And something else made her happy. Nothing would happen to her or her family. Maxim would protect them. They would all succeed in 'surviving into the peace', as Gisela had put it.

He was already wearing his uniform as he waited for her in the corridor. The military boots too. His beard didn't fit in with the uniform at all. But then he wouldn't be wearing that much longer.

She realised that he was extremely impatient. He had obviously believed that he would be able to leave the bunker immediately. But she made it clear to him that the Russians hadn't yet arrived. It wasn't a good idea to show himself in the village on his own yet. She made him understand: just another couple of hours, at most.

He laughed when she unpacked Seff's shaving things. Eagerly he made a small fire in the bright room, heated water, shaved. He looked at himself thoroughly in the mirror. In the last few months he had almost always only been able to see himself in water, and only in the light from the torch or by candlelight at that.

When he saw her unpacking the food from the rucksack, he became animated. He shook his head, stuffed it all back in again, took the rucksack and made signs to her to follow him. She stood still and signed to him too: Stay here! Wait! But he shook his head, laughed piercingly, pointed upwards. How loud he was all of a sudden! How his laughter echoed around the walls! He grabbed the cutlery, shoved it in one of his coat pockets, stowed the cup and plate in the other. What was he doing? She followed him into the corridor.

There he didn't head towards the entrance but deeper into the mountain. He walked like someone who knew his way, and he wasn't bothered when the corridors became gloomy.

They came to the shaft. Maxim threw Anna a triumphant glance and pointed to the staircase. With a bound he was on the third step, waved to her and reached out his hand to her. She jumped. On the steps she looked up and had to close her eyes, the light was so dazzling.

Maxim beat his arms, made movements like a bird flying upwards. Then he laughed again, loudly and boisterously. The echo droned around the shaft. Without his beard, in uniform, so loud that it sometimes hurt her ears – was this still the Maxim that she knew?

211

When they arrived at the top they were bathed in the warmth of the sun. They found themselves on the peak of a steep pile of concrete blocks. She had never ventured this far before. But he seemed to have been here several times. At dawn, or dusk, perhaps? Perhaps on a moonlit night?

It was certain that he had looked over the landscape from here, carefully, without moving much, without showing a suspicious silhouette. Just the scent of the forests, the colours, the wind, the light, and above all the enormous sky must have been overwhelming experiences for him.

From here you could see for miles over the landscape in two directions, just over the tops of the spruces. To the west lay Stiegnitz, embedded in a valley, behind it rose the spring green mountain slopes. To the east lay Mellersdorf, in a low valley. Both villages appeared to have died out, nothing was moving. Further east still, rose dark clouds of smoke. Several villages over there were burning. Anna listened. She could no longer hear the thunder of artillery.

The road which led from Mellersdorf to Stiegnitz, around the edge of the forest, was lined with debris. The sun was reflected in the panels of the overturned cars, its light glinting up at them. The road was empty and dead, as far as the eye could see.

Maxim balanced on the edge of the shaft. He put his hands behind his head and stretched. Then he took the rucksack off and passed it to Anna. They sat down and Anna unpacked.

Maxim was glad to see the bottle of Sekt and the tin of caviar, and read the labels with shining eyes. Then he opened the bottle. It popped, the cork went flying, froth streamed out. He pulled the cup from his coat pocket, poured and passed it to Anna. He tried to drink out of the bottle himself. It sparkled. They toasted each other, she in German, he in Russian.

Timidly she took a sip. It tingled on her tongue! So that was what peace tasted like. She looked at Maxim, how happy he was. '*Mir*, Yeva, *mir*!' he cried and waved the bottle.

Despite all the joy and relief, there was bitterness in her now. And she didn't like this caviar, the little black balls out of a tin. She preferred Grandmother's sandwiches. She looked at him laughingly as he feasted on caviar, ate two sandwiches and then half a bar of chocolate. He gave the other half to her. He tried a piece of cheese too. And the coffee.

It was no coffee substitute. And Grandmother hadn't skimped on the beans, hoarded for bad times. The coffee was as strong as on a feast day. It made them both wide-awake, and the Sekt had such an effect on Anna that she felt as if she was lifted out of all the bitterness. It was a holiday, in spite of everything! Peace deserved to be celebrated. And the fact that they were both still alive. Long live life!

She thought briefly of Gisela. Had she been able to survive? That wasn't a foregone conclusion. She could have been caught on her flight between the fronts or in one of the last bombing raids.

Dear God, let her still be alive, thought Anna. Let her have survived into the peace!

Maxim took off the uniform coat and undid the buttons on his tunic. Anna slipped out of her coat too and hung it over a rusty steel beam which stuck up vertically from the rubble. She felt like a butterfly which had just slipped out of its cocoon. Her hair waved in the wind. She showed Maxim her photos: Felix, Seff, Grandmother, Mother and Father. It was so good to be able to speak to each other loudly, carefree, like in peacetime in fact. Maxim pointed to Father's photo, then to Anna, pointed here and there – to the eyes, the mouth, the curly hair. Then he pulled out the photo of his family, held it in the sunlight and kissed it.

The air smelled of resin, of moss and budding leaves. Maxim pointed to a buzzard, circling above them, and began to hum, then to sing, he bellowed out a song with a rousing rhythm and a catchy tune.

Anna soon picked it up and hummed along. As she mastered the melody, he improvised a harmony and accompanied her. He jumped up and pulled her up too and then they tried to dance on the narrow platform of rubble. Her red dress flapped. They both had to take care not to fall off. Anna thought briefly: really, an unbelievable scene. She was quite beside herself with life.

214

22

In the middle of this whirl, she cast her eye over the landscape beyond Mellersdorf, and saw a military column appear, still a long way off. She stopped and showed Maxim. 'Russians,' she said.

He laughed and whooped, waved and shouted. But the soldiers were far too far away, they couldn't possibly see him yet.

Now all of a sudden, he was in a tearing hurry. Hastily he pulled on his coat and packed the crockery and leftovers in the rucksack. Anna got ready quickly too. With the rucksack on his back, he descended the steps first and gave her his hand, as she shuddered at the thought of the dark abyss below the steps.

They hurried down the corridor, briefly returned to the rooms in which Maxim had stayed for five months, paused there only to pull the pins out of the map, fold it up, pack it away.

Anna looked around her. He had already cleaned the cutlery and placed it together, had rolled the duvet up in the rag rug, laid the quilt on top. Herr Beranek's clothes lay next to it, neatly folded. It was too much for them to be able to take it all down with them now. And Anna was in a hurry. She made Maxim understand that the things should stay here for now, until the situation down there had calmed down.

And Maxim seemed hardly able to wait any longer to be with his own people. They rushed to the exit. They ran over the dandelion meadows in front of the bunker and walked through the forest, which was already casting long shadows, down the slope, side by side. The sun stood over the peak of the western mountains. There was an hour at most until it set, after a glorious spring day.

Below them lay the village in the evening sun. The sounds of motors, men's voices penetrated up to them. So the Russians were already in Stiegnitz. Faster, faster! Maxim panted. No wonder. He'd hardly moved for the last five months and had never had enough to eat. Anna offered to carry the rucksack, but he declined.

As they came out of the forest, she pointed to the low hill opposite: there, the farm! She pointed to herself, pointed to the buildings again. He nodded. There he had crawled into the barn, more dead than alive, five months ago.

Was Mother at home? She had probably preferred to stay in the Lamb, to prevent looting and to be close to Hedi's children. Were Grandmother and Felix sitting together in the living room? No, Felix would be bound to be upstairs, standing behind the curtains in the boys' room, peering out.

Why, for heaven's sake, wasn't there a sheet hanging from the gables?

They crossed the bridge and hurried up the hill, towards the farm. A babble of Russian voices sounded from one of the houses in the direction of the village. Anna saw that Maxim was listening open-mouthed, and was thankful to realise that he didn't turn off in that direction, but stayed at her side. He seemed to know very well that she and her family urgently needed his protection and support, although he was powerfully drawn towards his countrymen, his comrades.

He would position himself outside the front door and vigorously turn away any looters, any men looking for women: Not here! Keep your hands off this family, this house! Someone lives here who saved my life!

But now three Russians came, laughing and loud, out of a house down there, the first house over the bridge. One had an arm full of bottles, another was carrying an oil painting. Maxim stood still and waved to them. They called something out to him, he answered. At the same time he put his hand on Anna's shoulder. With astonished sounding exclamations, the soldiers hurried up the slope towards Maxim. Their faces beamed. Maxim threw his arms in the air with a shout of joy.

At that moment, Felix stormed out of the house.

'It's all right, Felix,' cried Anna. 'It's Maxim!'

Maxim turned to face him in astonishment. It was only now that Anna realised that Felix had a rifle in his hand. His face was distorted with rage.

'So!' he roared. 'It was all lies!' As fast as lightning he aimed and shot, before Maxim could even throw himself down.

'No!' screamed Anna, horrified.

There were three bangs. Maxim fell on his back. One shot had hit his brow, another his throat. He lay on the rucksack, his head hung down over the blankets. A thick jet of blood shot from the wound in his throat.

Anna fell silent.

'Traitor!' she heard Felix say, right next to her.

She stared at the red puddle with hanging arms.

Maxim was dead.

Everything was happening so fast, it was getting faster and faster. Grandmother came running out of the house, screaming. Noises were approaching from below too. The roar of Russian voices. Anna saw Grandmother trying to tear the rifle away from Felix. 'But he's just a child!' she screamed, over and over. 'But he's just a child!'

Shots whistled over Anna's head. She threw herself to the ground, lay on Maxim, saw Felix keel over and fall, saw Grandmother collapse.

Someone grabbed her by the hair and pulled her away from Maxim, someone pulled her up and let her fall again. She lost consciousness.

As she came to, she saw firelight, heard crackling.

Flames were shooting from the broken living room windows.

Glossary

Blutwurst – Blood sausage, equivalent to black pudding.

Erzgebirge – A mountain range on the border between Germany and the Czech Republic, formerly rich in mineral resources.

'From the Maas to Memel, from the Etsch to the Belt' – Line from the first stanza of the German national anthem (the only one used during the Nazi period), defining the limits of German territory. Written at a time when the Rivers Maas (Meuse), Memel, Etsch (Adige) and Belt (part of the Baltic) were the approximate borders of the area where German was spoken. and would have been the borders if Germany had been unified at that time.

Führer – While this title, which literally means 'leader' is well known as the one adopted by Hitler, it was also used by leaders at all levels of the party and the Hitler Youth. In the girls' organisations, the feminine form *Führerin* was used, the plural of which is *Führerinnen*.

German Girls' League (*Bund Deutscher Mädel*) – The Hitler Youth organisation for girls aged 14–18. Here the girls were indoctrinated into the Nazi ideology through various activities and political training. Although they were supposed to be prepared for a life where their responsibilities were restricted to *Kinder*, *Küche*, *Kirche* (children, kitchen, church), they were also expected to take part in sports and physical training. The groups had a similar structure to the Nazi party and the leaders were given militaristic titles (see *Führer*).

Gröfaz – Contraction of *Grosster Führer aller Zeiten*: literally 'the Greatest Leader of all Time', used ironically of Hitler, but now also of any leader – The Big Boss.

Hitler Youth (*Hitlerjugend*) – All children were required to join a Hitler Youth organisation on 20 April (Hitler's birthday) of the year they turned ten, after passing an initiation test called the *Pimpfenprobe*. The oath was 'I promise as a member of the Hitler Youth always to do my duty with love and loyalty to *Führer* and flag'. Boys aged 10–14 joined the *Jungvolk* (Young Folk), and girls the *Jungmädel* (Young Girls), before moving up to the *Bund Deutscher Mädel* and *Hitlerjugend*.

Jud Süss – 1940 propaganda film, director: Veit Harlan. A historical melodrama about an evil Jewish businessman, Süss Oppenheimer, treasurer to the corrupt Duke of Württemburg.

Ohm Krüger – 1941 film, director: Hans Steinhoff. Tells the story of Paul Krüger, and the Boer War from a strongly anti-British stance.

People's Radios (*Volksempfänger*) – Mass-produced radio sets, among the cheapest in Europe. They were subsidised by the Nazi regime to make sure that as many people as possible could afford them and hear the speeches by Hitler and other Nazi leaders which were broadcast on them.

Pimpf – Literally means 'lad'. Youngest member of the *Jungvolk*. Plural – *Pimpfe*.

Ruhrgebiet – Germany's main industrial and coalmining region, around the valley of the River Ruhr in North Rhine-Westphalia, including the cities of Düsseldorf, Duisberg, Essen and Dortmund.

School grades – in German schools, pupils do not get graded A, B, etc, but from 1 (the best) to 5 (the worst).

Sekt – German sparkling wine, equivalent to champagne.

Service (*Dienst*) – Obligation to share in meetings and obey the orders of the Nazi party and its organisations.

Sudetenland – This area is on the border between Germany and what is now the Czech Republic, and was granted to Czechoslovakia at the end of the First World War because of its strategic location. However, it had a predominantly German population, and was annexed by Germany after the Munich Conference in 1938. This was followed in March 1939 by the German occupation of the rest of Czechoslovakia, which was called the 'Protectorate' as it was under German protection but not part of the Reich itself.

Volkssturm – Equivalent to Home Guard, introduced in October 1944 and made up of boys and old men.

Warthegau – Administrative district established by the Germans including Posen, Lodz and Warsaw. After the Polish campaign had ended, Poland was divided into three major sections: the former 'Polish corridor' was restored to West Prussia, the western third of Poland was dubbed 'Warthegau', and central Poland became the 'Government General for the Occupied Polish Territories' or General Government. West Prussia and the Warthegau ceased to be Polish territory and became part of the Reich, while the General Government was under civil administration.